MW00942551

The Bridge Murders

by

Merri Borkowski

authorHOUSE

1663 LIBERTY DRIVE, SUITE 200
BLOOMINGTON, INDIANA 47403
(800) 839-8640
www.authorhouse.com

First published by AuthorHouse 04/21/04

ISBN: 1-4184-0823-9 (e)
ISBN: 1-4184-0824-7 (sc)

Printed in the United States of America
Bloomington, Indiana

This book is printed on acid-free paper.

PROLOG

Bridgeville is a cozy town on the Western banks of the Iroquois River nestled in the cornfields of Central Illinois. It got its name from the fact that in the pioneer days, the only bridge across the river for 20 miles in either direction was at this point. A town grew up around the western edge of the bridge and soon people were referring to the town as Bridgeville. It grew rapidly until a flourmill was built on the eastern shore to take advantage of the waterpower to turn the mill. Workers moved across the river to live near their work. Soon Milltown grew to be larger than Bridgeville and it has remained so to this day despite the fact that Cycle Card Company moved its playing card manufacturing plant to Bridgeville in 1900.

Bridgeville is a friendly town where neighbors share their lives – the good times and the bad. Usually the good times outweighed the bad; usually, that is until dead bodies started turning up.

Chapter 1

"One Club."

"Two Hearts."

"Two Hearts? Oh, that's a jump shift. She must have lots of points. What should I bid?" wondered Jenny. "I'll bet Peggy bids a short club and my hand isn't very good. What should I do? I don't think we should be any higher, but I don't have enough hearts to support her. Oh, I wish I knew what to do."

"Pass," said Jenny.

"Four Hearts," responded Molly Donner.

"Pass." "Pass" "Pass"

"Looks like they're your hearts, Connie," said Molly as she pushed her chair away from the table. "Might as well take this time as dummy to freshen the drinks," decided Molly as she got the pitcher from the kitchen.

She checked the table here on the three-season porch and the one in the living room by the field stone fireplace. No fire today with its crisp, fall weather, but soon the beautiful multicolored leaves will have fallen from the trees and a fire will warm the room from the thick cream colored carpet to the hand-hewn beams in the ceiling.

"Looks like we need more trailmix here," she said as she poured more iced tea into Angie O'Connor's glass. "Will you fill up the bowls while I add more ice?"

The Tuesday Bridge Club was finishing their fourth hand and were about to change places again to their next assigned seat as dictated by their tally cards. These eight women had been playing bridge on the third Tuesday of the month for the past 20 years. Early on when many of them were working and they had small children at home, they played on Tuesday evening. But now that most of them were retired, they played in the afternoon. They knew each other about as well as anyone could. They'd comforted each other through deaths, divorce, and even a flood. They celebrated graduations, weddings, and births of grandchildren.

Only three of the original members had been replaced. Angie O'Connor was the first replacement. She and her husband, Brian, came to Bridgeville 14 years ago from Carbondale where she was a successful real estate broker. She decided to open her own office in Bridgeville and over the years had bought and sold most of the stately old Victorian homes there as well as selling many of the newer ones in subdivisions sprouting up just outside of town. Connie Ryan joined the group after she and her husband opened The Four Aces restaurant on River Road near the bridge to Milltown. And Beth Sheridan joined them after moving to Bridgeville with her husband when they opened the Plush Pony, the clothing boutique.

Nora Beck turned to Beth and said, "Are you playing in the Last Gasp golf outing out at River Bend golf course on Thursday?"

"Sure. I wouldn't miss it," replied Beth. "Since I began lifting weights last spring with my personal trainer at the new health club, I've improved my swing 100 per cent. Jill Thomas, Pat Woods, Peggy Fitch, and I are a foursome. I just hope the weather is as nice as today since I'm having my hair done at Jenny's tomorrow."

"Are you guys finished in there?" shouted Jenny Wilcox from the three-seasons room. "We're ready to move."

After four more hands, the highlight of which was a small slam bid and played by Angie, the scores were totaled and the prizes awarded. As hostess, Molly was to decide what the prizes would be and which two places would receive them. She handed Angie a box of stationery wrapped in aqua tissue paper for finishing first and Jenny a smaller aqua package containing eight bridge tallies with Monet prints on the covers for coming in second.

"You can never have too many tallies," said Jenny. "Especially as often as we play marathons, party bridge and of course our Tuesday afternoons."

They gathered up their sweaters, purses, and car keys and headed for home backing carefully out of Molly's driveway to avoid hitting the truck parked across the road.

Chapter 2

He leaned against the tailgate of his truck a copy of Audubon's book, <u>Birds of North America</u>, in one hand and a pair of binoculars in the other. He decided to bring the book at the last minute just in case someone driving along River Road saw him parked there and wondered what he was doing. Bird watching was practically a religion in Bridgeville. No one would suspect that his real reason for being there was to catch a glimpse of Connie when she finished her bridge game and headed for home. He never would've known where to find her if he hadn't overheard her mention it to the cashier at Kroger's grocery store yesterday. He always did his shopping at 8:30 in the morning on Monday because often Connie was there at that time. He loved chatting with her as they poked and prodded the produce looking for the freshest ingredients for their upcoming meals. He was lucky his job was so flexible. Otherwise, he'd have to look for other ways to be near her.

Suddenly he heard Molly Donner's screen door slam and saw the ladies head for their cars. He looked through the binoculars searching for Connie's frosted hair. There she was climbing into that sporty little black car of hers and turning left toward town. Probably headed for home to cook supper for that husband of hers. As he watched her car turn the bend and disappear from sight, he wished she were hurrying home to cook for him.

Sighing, he got into his truck and pulled out onto River Road. Better get back to work before somebody missed him and started asking questions about where he'd been. As he drove along, he made up his mind to take bridge lessons the next time they offered them at the Adult Education evening classes. Any excuse to be near Connie. He thought about her day and night dreaming of the time when they would be together, longing for the time when their lives would be one.

Chapter 3

Angie stuck around after everyone else left to help Molly straighten up. They had become fast friends since Angie and Brian moved to Bridgeville when he was named Principal of Bridgeville High School where Molly and her husband Seth both taught. "What time do we tee off on Thursday?" Angie asked.

Looking at the calendar with large squares big enough to keep track of her busy life, Molly replied, "8:15."

"Good," said Angie. "I'm showing property at 2:30 to the wife of the new manager of Cycle Cards. They have four children so she's looking at homes here in town rather than those new ones out by the High School. The new homes are really nice but not nearly as roomy as the Victorians on Main Street and those down by the river. Have you ever considered selling your house, Molly?" she asked. "She might like this Tudor style."

"Since Seth died I have sort of rattled around in here, but I love living by the river and I really need the room when Ken, Kate, and their families visit."

"Well, if you ever change your mind, let me know. They're building some gorgeous condos over in Milltown right on the banks of the river. From the balconies on the second and third floors you can see all the way down to the bend. I was over there last week and the colors of the trees reflected on the water were breathtaking. What are you going to do about your leaves? You don't rake them all yourself, do you?"

"Goodness, no!" replied Molly. "With over an acre of oaks and maples, I wouldn't get done until Christmas. My son, Ken, and his family are coming over in a couple weeks on a Saturday to rake. His wife, Sandy, and I rake for a while and then come inside to get ready to roast hot dogs over the burning leaves. It's become almost a ritual the last few years. We've been doing this since the boys were in the Upper Grade Center. It's really a fun tradition. The only hard part is keeping Blondie, their golden lab, from jumping in the piles of leaves and scattering them all over the yard again."

"Sounds like fun to me," said Angie. "Do you put this good china in the dishwasher?"

"Yes, but I do the silver by hand. It gives me a chance to unwind and think about some of the hands I played this afternoon and wonder how I would have played them differently."

"Well, I wouldn't want to interrupt your reverie," said Angie. "Brian and I both have an evening at home tonight so I put a roast in the oven before I left. It's so tender when it's cooked long and slow. And I love the way the carrots, onions, and potatoes taste when they're cooked with the roast."

"Me too," said Molly. "And served with a loaf of that crusty bread they have at the bakery, it makes a wonderful meal."

"Crusty bread! Good idea! If I leave now I'll just have time to get to the bakery before they close. Bye. See you Thursday. Thanks for the stationery!" and with that Angie banged out the screen door, hopped into her cherry red Catera and roared off down the driveway, crunching leaves as she went.

Chapter 4

Alone at last, Molly decided to start the dishwasher, put the silver to soak in some hot, soapy water in the sink and go for a walk while the light was still good. She'd put the card tables and chairs away later. For now, she'd put on her cable knit sweater and her old tennis shoes and go scuffing through the leaves on the path to the woods down by the river. "Oh, how I love Fall!" she said out loud hoping no one would hear her talking to herself.

"What a fun group," she thought as she strolled along. "I've known so many of them all my life. Nora looks the same today as she did in the 7th grade. Her golden pageboy is still shiny and smooth except now there are a few gray hairs mixed in with the blond ones. And when she strides along on those long legs of hers, her hair still swings easily back and forth."

Oh, those 7th grade days when Nora's father was President of the Bridgeville National Bank and Molly's father was the President of the Cycle Card Company. How many afternoons Nora and Molly spent sitting in the large swing down by the river sharing secrets and dreams. They had remained such good friends all through high school only to part ways when Molly went to Northern Illinois University to enroll in education courses and Nora went to Swathmore, Pennsylvania, to study Art. Both married and returned to Bridgeville where Molly's husband became the Business Teacher and basketball coach at the High School and Nora's husband went to work in the bank where he worked his way up to the Presidency filling her father's shoes when he retired.

Molly paused on her way back to the house to sit in the gazebo for a few minutes to watch the sunset. "Screening this in was the smartest thing we ever did," she thought. "I remember the day Seth and Ben did it."

Emily Grant's husband, Ben, owned the hardware store in town. He and Seth had played on the basketball team together in high school. Now the Grants lived right next door to the Donners. What a handy neighbor. No matter what tool Seth had needed, Ben had it. Over the years those two had put up swing sets, screened in porches, remodeled bathrooms and built enough sets for the local playhouse to last a lifetime. Emily and Molly had taught together for 30 years--Molly teaching English and Emily teaching P. E. You could still see Emily every summer down at the community pool teaching Bridgeville youngsters how to swim. She and Molly were like two peas in a pod with their black-turning-gray hair cut short and curling around their faces, their short, stocky bodies, their soft gray eyes and their easy smiles. When Angie first came to town, she thought Molly and Emily were sisters. They finally became related through marriage. Their children's marriage that is.

Chapter 5

Kate Donner and Doug Grant were as different as their mothers were alike. Kate was tall and slim with hair as flaming red as her Grandpa Sean's and a temper to match (although Grandpa Sean would never have called it a temper. He always described his personality as having a "singleness of purpose.") Doug was about the same height as Kate, but his hair was black and curly like his mother's and he had the broad shoulders and narrow waist of a swimmer.

Kate was a starting forward on the girls' basketball team; Doug swam the butterfly on the swim team. Kate was on student government; Doug was on the debate team. Kate was a Thespian; Doug played baseball. If there was an activity at Bridgeville High, one or the other was involved. After graduating from high school, both attended the University of Illinois and both went on to law school there. Kate and two friends from Presby Hall, where she lived as an undergrad, moved into a house on Florida Avenue to be closer to the law building. Doug moved from the Sigma Chi house on John Street to the luxury dorms on Daniel Street. It was the first time in their lives that they had lived more than a few hundred yards apart.

Graduation day from law school found them both headed for jobs in St. Louis. Doug was going to work for Shultz and

Donovan as a tax attorney while Kate was employed as a corporate attorney for Anhuiser Bush. They considered moving in together but decided their parents would never approve. So on July 4, they invited their friends and relatives to gather at the park under the Arch in St. Louis and in this city where the Missouri River and the Mississippi River join together to become one, Doug and Kate got married.

Molly and Seth and Emily and Ben were delighted. Since the day they moved in next door to each other, Kate and Doug had been good friends. Racing each other from the dock to the raft moored in the river, playing hide and seek around the gazebo and in the woods between their houses, and competing at video games to see who could shoot more aliens than the other, they were inseparable. Marriage seemed like the logical conclusion to this life-long friendship.

Chapter 6

As Molly sat reminiscing, the sun sank slowly behind her. "Better go in and do those dishes," she thought as she stood up and walked toward the house. She went into the kitchen and headed for the sink. As she dipped her hands with their sturdy thumbs into the warm, sudsy water she thought about her dad. "Molly Magee," he would say. "You could do anything with those sturdy thumbs." And she really could. She loved to bake bread, plant the garden, arrange flowers, play the organ in church, and most of all hold the cards while she played bridge. She slowly washed each piece of her good silver, rinsed it and laid it carefully on the tea towel on the counter. Then drying each piece separately, she placed them into the silver chest closing the lid tightly so that they would stay bright and shiny for the next time it was her turn to entertain. She folded up the card tables and the folding chairs and put them back in the closet near the garage. She put the cards and score books back in the octagonal table between the two brown plaid recliners by the fireplace in the living room. "Done!" she thought to herself. "Think I'll warm up a little of that cheese soup left over from lunch and see what kind of sandwiches are left over."

The Tuesday Bridge Club met eight times a year from September to May (with time out in December because everyone was so busy preparing for the holidays) for lunch and bridge. The hostess would furnish a big pot of hearty soup, beverages, and some nibbles to munch on during the game. Each woman would bring her favorite sandwich cut into quarters. All the sandwiches would be laid out buffet-style on the kitchen counter along with plates, bowls, napkins, soupspoons and the crockpot of soup. As they went down the line, each would take a bowl of soup, a quarter of her own sandwich and a quarter of three other sandwiches so they could have a variety of tastes. Molly usually brought ham, lettuce, tomato, provolone cheese and mayo on homemade sourdough bread. Angie's favorite was chicken salad on a croissant. Connie liked bean sprouts, lettuce, tomato, chopped cucumbers mixed with ranch dressing and rolled up in lavash bread. Nora could be counted on to bring thinly sliced grilled chicken breast, leaf lettuce, vinaigrette dressing on toasted rye bread. Beth loved bbq chicken on an onion roll. Peggy often brought cold meatloaf with Dijon mustard on white bread. Emily liked bacon, lettuce, and tomato on toast. And Jenny's favorite was a Rueben complete with corned beef, sauerkraut, Swiss cheese, Thousand Island dressing on pumpernickel bread. No one ever went home hungry.

Molly took her soup, a few slices of Jonathan apple, and the last quarter of a Jenny's Rueben sandwich and sat down at the kitchen table to eat and read the paper. After supper, she unloaded the dishwasher, put her supper things in, and went out to the garage to put her golf clubs in the trunk of her tan Taurus. She'd have to go out to the driving range tomorrow to hit a few balls and practice her putting. She hadn't played golf for about a month because she'd been busy organizing the church bazaar.

"I sure don't want to embarrass the others in the foursome," she thought as she sank down in the steaming hot bath water. "Nothing like a hot bath and a good book to read in bed to wind up a really great day."

Just as she stepped out of the tub, the phone rang. She put on her robe and hurried into the bedroom wrapping her wet hair in a towel as she went.

14

"Hello," she said as she grabbed the phone on the fourth ring just before the answering machine took over.

"Hi, Mom. This is Kate."

"Well, hi. How are you?" asked Molly. "How do the kids like school this year?

"They're doing just great." replied Kate. "Bridgette's teacher is Mrs. O'Hara. She told Bridgette that her birthday is on St. Patrick's Day just like Bridgette's. Bridgette asked her if they ate corned beef and cabbage to celebrate and Mrs. O'Hara said of course they did. What else would you eat on St. Patrick's Day? Brad's first grade teacher is Mrs. Krelowitz. He remembered her from three years ago when she was Bridgette's teacher. He felt right at home in her room. Hey, how was your bridge game today? Did you win first prize?"

"No. I was Angie's partner, though, when she bid and made a small slam. We had a lot of fun and the sandwiches were great."

"What kind of soup did you make?" asked Kate.

"Canadian Cheese," replied Molly. "You know the kind with the little pieces of cauliflower in it. I think you gave me the recipe."

"I love that. Do you have any left? I think Doug and the kids and I will be up there this weekend. It's Doug's dad's birthday and we always like to be in on the celebration."

"I don't have any soup left, but I have the ingredients to make more. I've been invited to the party, too. Why don't I take that as my dish to pass?" said Molly.

"Great idea. Doug's mom is having steaks on the grill. I'm planning to bring baked beans."

"Are you making those I like with brown sugar, BBQ sauce, green peppers and lots of onions?" asked Molly.

"Yep. Those are the very ones. You know we have such fun at those family gatherings that Doug and I are thinking about moving back to Bridgeville. He'd have to give up his partnership at

Shultz and Donovan, but maybe we could open an office together. I'm going stir crazy now that both kids are in school all day."

"That would be wonderful! I'm anxious to hear more about it on Saturday," exclaimed Molly as she grabbed the towel that was beginning to slip off her head. "Listen, I just got out of the tub when you called and I'm standing here in a towel. I'd better hang up and get ready for bed. "

"I'll see you Saturday. Bye. I love you, Mom." said Kate.

"Love you too, honey. Give Doug and the kids a big hug for me." said Molly as she hung up. "Thank goodness we don't have phones where you can see the party on the other end," she thought as she put on her nightgown and fluffed her wet hair with a towel.

The next morning she got up bright and early, grateful that she had set the automatic coffeepot last night. It was so nice to wake up to that coffee smell drifting up the stairs and into her bedroom. Sliding into her fuzzy red robe and comfy slippers, she shuffled down the stairs and into the kitchen. Soon she was munching a toasted bagel slathered with peach preserves and sipping on coffee trying not to scald her tongue.

"I'd better call Beth to remind her that I'm going to pick up the proceeds from the bazaar and deposit them in the bank this morning." The phone rang and rang but no one answered. "Darn," she thought, "if she's not at home, the least she could do is put her answering machine on. Where could she be so early? Maybe she's in the shower. I'll just have to take my chances at catching her later."

Kate's Cheddar Cheese and Cauliflower Soup

Serving Size : 4

4 Tbs. Butter
3 medium carrots, diced into small pieces
3 medium celery stalks diced into small pieces
1 medium onion minced
3 Tbs. Flour
1 ½ cups Chicken stock or canned chicken broth
½ small Cauliflower, trimmed and cut into very small pieces
8 oz. Mild Cheddar Cheese, grated (2 cups plus)
1 ½ cups Half and half
¼ tsp. Cayenne pepper
1 tsp. Salt

Heat the butter in a large sauce pan. Add the carrots, celery, and onions and sauté for about 5 minutes until the vegetables are soft. Stir in the flour and cook over low heat until flour is incorporated (about 1 minute).

Stirring constantly, gradually add stock and then the cauliflower. Bring to a boil and simmer until the cauliflower is tender (about 5 minutes). Stir in the grated cheese and cook for about 30 seconds until the cheese is melted. (Do not bring soup to a boil after cheese is added or the soup will break.) Turn down the heat and add the half and half. Cook over low heat stirring until smooth. Season with salt and pepper.

[COOKS Magazine; Oct 1989]

Posted by Fred Peters.

Chapter 7

The church bells were chiming 6:00 as Beth walked down her sidewalk on her way to The Clip Joint to have Jenny Wilcox do her hair. As she neared the street, she heard the phone ringing. Who would be calling this early? Oh well, whoever it was would call back. The last time she had her hair cut, Jenny suggested highlighting it to cover up the gray that was just beginning to show up. She didn't want to be late because Jenny had done her a favor by squeezing her in early this morning. Beth turned left at the end of her sidewalk, crossed the street, and walked down the block to Jenny's shop.

"Good morning," said Jenny. "Ready for a new look?"

"Ready as I'll ever be," responded Beth. "Steve'll be so surprised when he gets back from New York on Saturday."

"Well, if he doesn't like it, we can always change it back," said Jenny as she wrapped the vinyl throw around Beth's shoulders and ran her hands through her short curly hair.

"Looks like your perm turned out nice," said Jenny.

"Yea, I hope the frosting is as successful," replied Beth

Chapter 8

Molly had to stop at the church on her way to the golf course to pick up the items that didn't sell at the bazaar. One of the things on her "to do list" today was to return these items to the people who donated them.

"We'll probably see them back here again next year," she thought as she backed out of the driveway.

As she neared the church, she smiled to herself thinking how many years she'd been attending this church. Bible school when she was little. Sunday School and church services all through elementary and high school. Playing the organ in the summer while the regular organist took some time off. Her wedding day. Singing in the choir. And now EX-chairman of the annual bazaar.

"Hello, Reverend Brown!" Molly shouted as she entered the Gathering Room next to the sanctuary.

"Hello, Molly!" he shouted back from his study. She heard his footsteps echoing in the sanctuary as he crossed the hardwood floor and entered the Gathering Room .

"Are you here for the bazaar items?" he asked.

"Yes," she said. "I've got to return them and deposit the proceeds in the bank. We made almost $2500 this year. Beth Sheridan took it home with her after the sale to count it and wrap the coins. I'm on my way now to pick up the money and take it to the bank. Are you playing in the Last Gasp golf tournament tomorrow?"

"Yes, my tee off time is not until noon, though. It's such a worthwhile cause. So many children in need of winter clothes both here and in Milltown. Can I help you load these things in your car?"

"No thanks. There are just a few and none of them is very heavy. Thanks anyway, though. See you tomorrow."

"What did she want?" asked Rick James, the janitor and handyman around the church. "More bazaar stuff? She about drove me crazy the last couple weeks. She was here 24-7 and always asking for things. 'Rick could you set up the tables in the hall for me?' 'Rick could you move the tables around for me?' 'Rick, Rick, Rick.' Couldn't she do anything herself? I never did like her even when I had her as a teacher in the tenth grade after my folks moved here from Decatur. She was always on my case about something. She didn't think I was smart enough to go to college, but I showed her."

"Really? I didn't know you went to college." said Rev. Brown.

"Yea, but I quit in my sophomore year and joined the Army. Being stationed in France was the best thing that ever happened to me. I learned a lot in the Army. While I was in France, I even dated a French girl. She called me 'Reeshard.' I thought about calling myself that when I got back to the U. S. but decided not to cause everybody would think I was trying to put on airs."

"Well, education is never wasted. Whatever you learned I'm sure it made you what you are today."

"Yea, a handyman that's only good enough to move tables wherever those bossy women want them."

"Now, Rick," said Rev. Brown. "Be charitable. Those women worked hard to make money for the church. Why, they raised enough to buy a new computer. It will be so much easier

22

for Mrs. Pemberton to get the weekly bulletin and the monthly newsletter out using a computer instead of her old typewriter."

"How much did those old broads make anyway?" asked Rick.

"About $2500 Mrs. Donner thought. She's on her way to Mrs. Sheridan's house right now to find out for sure."

Chapter 9

Molly stopped at Mrs. Peabody's to drop off the crocheted doilies, continued down the block to return the hand painted ash trays with the bunnies on them to Mrs. Desmond ("I'll bet these were left over from the Easter bazaar at St. Mary's," she thought to herself. "Now Molly. That's not very charitable. Mrs. Desmond probably likes bunnies. Someone should tell her that since so many people have stopped smoking, the ashtrays don't sell.").

On her way to Mrs. Hazlett's to return the knitted potholders she stopped by Beth's to pick up the money. She knocked, rang the doorbell, even walked around to the kitchen door to see if anyone was at home. No answer. "I wonder where she can be," thought Molly as she peered through the glass in the kitchen door. "I told her yesterday that I would be here around ten o'clock. Oh, well, I'll stop by again after these last two stops."

Mrs. Ross lived right next door to Mrs. Hazlett so Molly quickly left the hand painted trays and the silk-screened tea towels with them and headed back to Beth's. After knocking and ringing the doorbell to no avail, she decided to stop again on her way home from the golf course. "Oops! I better get some gas or I won't be stopping by anywhere," she thought.

As Molly pulled up to the gas pumps at the Shell station, Jimmy Reed came out of the office. "Here," he said. "Let me do that for you. What beautiful weather we're having, huh? I'm trying to be outside as much as I can. Speaking of being outside. Are you playing in the Last Gasp golf outing tomorrow?"

"Yes, I am," replied Molly. "In fact, I'm on my way to the golf course right now to get in a little practice."

"You wouldn't by any chance need a caddy for tomorrow, would you?" asked Jimmy.

"I don't know. I hadn't thought about it," she said.

"I'm enrolled at ITT in Chicago for the second semester and I'm doing this job and any other jobs I can in order to earn the $2,000 I need to pay for my tuition. I'm working here tomorrow night, so I'll be free during the day if you could use me for a caddy. What time do you tee off?"

"Eight fifteen," she replied. "Come to think of it, I could use a good caddy. Walking is so much better for me than riding in the cart and I am getting too old to carry my clubs. Why don't you meet me at the golf course about eight o'clock tomorrow?"

"Gee, thanks, Mrs. Donner. I'll see you tomorrow."

Chapter 10

He'd just hide here in the woods and wait for her to tee off on the third tee. It was far enough from the clubhouse that no one would see them. The woods here jutted out near the fairway and the women's tee was placed so that if she hit the ball a little to the left, it would go straight into the woods. With any luck that would happen today.

On his way to work this morning, he'd seen her sleek black car turn into the golf course parking lot. "Must be doing a little practicing for tomorrow," he thought to himself. "She never did like to be unprepared even when we were in college together."

As Freshmen, they had almost every class together. The first day he had seen her walk into the classroom bouncing along the way many runners do, laughing with a friend, shaking her head so that her hair flipped around her face. What kind of color did they call that hair? Oh yea, frosted. It looked nothing like any frosting he'd ever seen and since his mother died when he was 7 years old, he'd done a lot of cooking for himself and his dad. But he had overheard the girls talking about it one day and that's what they called it – frosting.

She was very popular. He wanted to ask her out, but he was afraid she'd turn him down. He was extremely shy. Even though he was tall and broad shouldered, he was very thin. He had worn horned rimmed glasses since he was in the sixth grade and he hated them every minute of every day. So he just smiled at her when they made eye contact, but he didn't speak to her throughout the entire year.

After his last final, he packed his things and went to Decatur for the summer to work in his uncle's pizza parlor. No matter how many cute girls came in to get pizza that summer, he spent all his time dreaming about Connie Kelly.

When he got back to school in September, he went to his first class early. He always liked to sit in the front so that if the teacher called on him he could answer without shouting from the back of the room. As he settled into his desk, he glanced up to see who was sitting down in the desk next to his. He had to blink twice to be sure it was her. Connie. Connie Kelly was sitting next to him and was about to speak to him.

"Hi," she said. "How was your summer?"

He couldn't believe it. She was actually talking to him. Somehow he managed to answer. They chatted for a minute or two until a girl named Emily sat down on the other side of her. Connie turned to talk to Emily and that was the end of his conversation. All the way home he was walking on a cloud. She had actually talked to him. Maybe this year he would ask her out. After all, she did ask him how his summer went.

Three weeks later he heard that Peter, Paul, and Mary were coming to Champaign. He stood in line all night at the student union to be sure to get good tickets. When the ticket booth opened at 8:00 the following morning, he was 10th in line. He got two tickets in Row 5 of section A of the Assembly Hall. Thrilled with his purchase, he raced to Lincoln Hall to make it to his nine o'clock class. Connie was there when he got there, but the teacher started class just as he sat down and he didn't get a chance to talk to her. The teacher wanted to talk to him after class about his last paper – one of the most insightful she had ever read – and Connie was gone by the time Mrs. Wilson was through with him.

It was a long two days until the next class. He arrived early and was sitting in his place when she walked in. As she sat down he blurted out that he had two tickets for the Peter, Paul, and Mary concert on Saturday and would she like to go with him. Smiling that wonderful smile of hers where her whole fact lit up and her blue eyes twinkled she said she'd love to. Love to! Wow! He was thrilled. Good thing Mrs. Wilson didn't call on him that day because he hadn't heard a word she said. As class ended, he turned to Connie to talk to her again. Too late. Pete Ryan was already walking out the door with her. How did he get to her so quickly when he sat way in the back of the room? Oh well, at least Pete wouldn't be taking her to the concert.

The big day came. He wore the new shirt his aunt had given him for his birthday and his best khakis. He'd gained a little weight over the summer. He'd gone home after his Freshman year vowing to get in shape by running at least two miles a day. Not only would running get him in shape, but that way he would have something in common to talk to Connie about when school started in the Fall.

He picked her up at the Kappa house and they walked out to the Assembly Hall. They found their seats just minutes before the lights dimmed. It was great sitting so close to her, touching shoulders, and listening to Puff the Magic Dragon and If I Had A Hammer.

After the concert, the huge crowd surged out of the doors and back toward the main part of the campus. Connie agreed with him that a pizza at the Thunderbird sounded good. As they ate, they talked about his working in a pizza place and about running. It was a wonderful date. Everything he had imagined. When they finished their pizza, they walked around the corner and up the stairs of her house. It was about 12:30 so the couples weren't lined up at the door saying goodnight yet. Connie and he each said what a good time they'd had. He decided to wait until their next date to kiss her goodnight. No sense in rushing it. But there was to be no next date.

On Monday when he got to class, she was already there talking with Emily. Both were squealing with delight and examining her newest acquisitions —Pete Ryan's SAE fraternity pin. He couldn't believe it. When did that happen? He was so sure that he and she would be a couple, not Pete and she. He was mortified.

For the next several weeks, he just went through the motions. He could hardly think of anything but Connie. His grades suffered because even though he went to his classes, he spent most of the time lying on his bed staring at the ceiling. He lost the weight he'd worked so hard to gain. He saw her often but just couldn't think of anything to say to her. At Christmas time he decided to take his finals but not to return for the next semester. He just needed to find himself. He withdrew from school, packed his bags, said goodbye to his aunt and uncle and took off in his '55 Chevy to search for the real John Gagnon.

Chapter 11

Who would've thought that after moving to this jerkwater town of Bridgeville one of the first people he would come face to face with was Connie Kelly. Of course, she didn't recognize him. Over the years, he had worked hard physically and had gained both weight and muscle mass. Gone were the glasses. He now had his hair styled at a salon in Chicago instead of cut at the local barbershop. All in all, he was a new man complete with a new name.

He peered through the trees at the third tee. Where was she? How long would it take her to play two holes? Just then he spied her red windbreaker through the trees. The wind was blowing her hair all around. She still wore it short and fluffy and of course frosted. He closed his eyes remembering how it felt sitting close to her at that concert, longing to run his fingers through that frosted hair.

Whack! He heard the club hit the ball and then almost immediately his wish came true. The ball landed practically at his feet. And here she came crashing through the woods looking for it. His hand closed over the grip on his five iron as he crouched behind a huge fir tree. He could see the red jacket getting closer. As she leaned down to pick up her ball, he sprang out from behind the evergreen holding the club up over his head. If he couldn't *have her, Pete Ryan couldn't have her either. Hearing the noise she glanced up just as he brought the club down with brutal force. It hit her just above the left eyebrow shattering her forehead, blood rushing down her face. She dropped to the pine-needle covered ground.*

"Oh, no," he thought as he looked down at the badly smashed face. "That's not Connie. Who the hell is it?"

He ran over to the third tee, hopped onto her cart and drove it into the woods. Spying a plastic airline ticket attached to the handle of her golf bag he read, "Beth Sheridan. 424 E. Polk Street. Bridgeville, IL."

"Oh no! Not Beth!" he thought. "Now what do I do?"

He ran back to his truck that was parked on the service drive which circled around the edge of the course. He grabbed a blanket from the back seat and ran back to the body. Good. Still no one in sight. He wrapped Beth's body in the blanket, carried it to his truck, and placed it carefully in the back seat. He ran back into the woods to get her clubs and spread some leaves over the blood on the ground. He slid his five iron into Beth's golf bag, slung it over his shoulder, and ran back to his truck. He put the clubs into the back, unzipped the pouch on the bag searching for her keys. Placing them in his pocket, he slammed the tail gate shut, got behind the wheel, started the engine, and put his head down on the steering wheel.

"What have I done?" he asked himself.

No time to think of that now. He had to get her back to her house before it got any later and her neighbors were up moving around.

He put the truck in gear and drove carefully south on River Drive. The light was green at the corner of River and Bridge Street. He went through the intersection to the alley behind Beth's house. He pulled into the driveway and left the motor running. Using Beth's keys to unlock the garage door, he went inside and pushed the button to activate the automatic garage door opener. He got back behind the steering wheel, pulled into the garage, and *closed the door.   Sliding the blanket-covered body from the back seat, he carried it through the garage and into the kitchen.   Good thing she was so little.   Even then she was getting heavy.   He laid her down on the floor in the dining room between the table and the buffet so that she couldn't be seen from the front door or the kitchen door.   He started opening drawers throwing stuff around on the floor to simulate a robbery.   Pulling open the middle drawer of the desk, he found $2000 in bills and several rolls of coins.*

"Why would she keep so much money just lying around?" he wondered as he stuffed the money in his pocket.

He dropped Beth's keys on the kitchen counter next to the sink, took the blanket off Beth's body, and went back to his truck for the clubs.   As he slid the clubs toward him, the phone in Beth's kitchen began to ring.   Startled, he quickly stood the golf bag in the corner, got back in his truck, and backed out of the garage.   He saw the light on in the kitchen of the house across the alley from Beth's.

"I sure hope nobody saw me leave," he thought.   "Maybe they'll think it's Beth going somewhere early."

He had to go somewhere and lie down for a while.   He couldn't go to work in this condition.   He was beginning to shake so much that he could hardly drive.   He headed south on Route 45 to the Stardust Motel.   He got the key from the office, unlocked the door of number 5, and flopped down on the bed.

"Just an hour or so and I'll be fine.   I've got to pull myself together."

He woke up forgetting where he was at first.   Then it all came flooding back.   He splashed cold water on his face, checked to see if he had any blood on his clothes, and left the motel room.   Tomorrow was the Last Gasp golf outing at the golf course.   The town would be crawling with golfers. They were going to be busier than ever at work tomorrow and he would surely be missed.   He hoped that that busybody who lived behind Beth didn't recognize his truck as he pulled out of Beth's driveway earlier.

"I'll have to take my truck in and get it detailed. Sure don't want anyone spying blood on the seats," he thought as he pulled away from the motel.

Chapter 12

Rick James slid his 6'2" frame behind the wheel of Rev. Brown's car pushing the seat back as he did so. Good thing the job at the church was flexible. He always had so many personal things to take care of on the side. A regular 9:00 – 5:00 job would really cramp his style.

As he adjusted the mirrors he hoped Rev. Brown would remember to readjust them the next time he drove. Rev. Brown was a nice enough guy but sometimes when he was driving his mind was out in left field somewhere. Slowly he backed out of Rev. Brown's garage, turned the corner and carefully pulled out into traffic. "I can't believe I'm driving this beater car," he thought. "I sure hope nobody I know sees me. Driving a station wagon is bad enough. Driving a rusty one is even worse. Add the Honk If You Love Jesus bumper sticker and it's the pits."

He turned left on Sheffield Street skirting the downtown shopping district hoping to avoid seeing his friends, parked in the municipal parking lot behind Penney's, and walked into the back door of Micky's Arcade. Moose and Sid were playing 8-ball, Jerry D was pounding on a pinball machine over in the corner, and Micky was behind the bar slicing buns and arranging cold cuts on a platter for lunchtime sandwiches. The Arcade didn't officially serve food, but Micky liked to have fixings for sandwiches for a few loyal customers to go along with the chips and pop they could get out of the machines lined up against the wall next to the video games. Pool was the game of choice for morning and early afternoon customers, but once school let out, the video games were the big draw.

"Hey, Micky. Ya seen Maurice around?" Rick yelled as he walked toward the bar.

He sat down and wrapped his long legs around the stool, leaning forward to rest his elbows on the bar. He peered through the gloom at the man behind the bar. He knew it was Micky by his voice, but he really couldn't see him very well without his glasses on. He hated wearing glasses ever since the kids in elementary school called him four eyes.

"Haven't seen him today. He was here yesterday for a while. Said he was on his way to Naperville to make a collection," Micky said as he reached for some tomatoes to slice.

"Well, I'll hook up with him later. I've got some money to pay on my account," said Rick as he climbed off the stool and headed toward the door.

"Damn!" he thought as he walked to the car. "Better get to Northend Garage to see if my truck's ready. I don't want to drive Rev. Brown's old rent-a-wreck any longer than I have to."

He slid behind the wheel, reached in his pocket for the keys, and felt the big wad of bills there. He took it out and counted it again glancing about nervously to be sure no one was watching. Twenty-five hundred dollars. What luck. He could pay off Maurice, get his truck fixed, and even have a few extra bucks left over. Maybe he'd make a few side bets on the golf game tomorrow. Most of the players were just hackers, but there were a few that might make it interesting. He'd talk to Maurice about it if he saw him tonight. If he won enough on the golf game, he might consider buying a new car. He liked his Ford pickup. He kept it shined up just like new. In fact, he had added a topper to cover the bed so that it would like one of those Suburbans, but in his mind he knew it was just a pickup. A buddy of his had a Suburban that was really sweet. Northend had one on the lot, but it was tan and he hated tan. Why would anyone buy a tan car? Maybe they could get him a dark blue one or that great dark green. Yea, that's what he wanted. Dark Green. If he didn't pay off Maurice, he could use the money in his pocket to put a down payment on the Suburban. No, better not. Everybody in town would wonder where he got the money for a new car. And Maurice was not one to wait for payment.

He was thinking so hard about the Suburban that he wasn't paying attention to his driving. He screeched to a halt just as a car went through the intersection with its horn blaring and its driver waving his fist out the window.

"Gotta be careful. Sure don't want to have to spend any money getting this heap fixed," he thought. He drove six more blocks to Northend Garage and parked next to the tan Suburban. He took the wad of bills out of his pocket, counted out $300, and put them in his wallet, stuffing the wad back into his pocket. He didn't want Jake to see him with all that money. He might find something else wrong with the truck if he thought Rick had more money.

"Hey, Jake," he said. "Is my truck ready?"

"No, besides cleaning it out we had to replace the brake shoes and the rotors. It's taking a lot longer than we thought. Check back with us later this afternoon or early tomorrow morning."

"Damn!" Rick said. "How long can it possibly take to do a brake job? I'm sick of waiting. Now I have to drive this piece of junk another day! I can't believe it! You guys are just stringing this out so you can charge me more."

He stormed out of the dealership slamming the door on his way out. He stomped to the car, got in, slammed the car door, and roared off down the street narrowly missing Molly who was just pulling out of the gas station.

Chapter 13

Pulling out of the gas station, Molly had to stop suddenly to avoid being run down by Rev. Brown's trusty old station wagon.

"Good thing he usually drives slowly," she thought to herself, "or he'd have killed half the population of Bridgeville by now. Why doesn't he watch where he is going?"

Arriving at the golf course, she spied Angie coming out of the pro shop. "Getting a little practice before the big day?" asked Angie.

"Yes, I'm so rusty. I didn't want to embarrass myself or the others in our foursome," replied Molly. "What are you doing for lunch? I hear the new chef here is outstanding."

"Sounds good to me," said Angie. "I'll meet you back here about 11:30. That way we'll beat the noon rush. Will that give you enough time?"

"Oh, that'll be plenty of time. I'll see you then."

Molly reached into her trunk and took the driver and the putter out of her golf bag. "No sense in hauling the whole bag out," she thought.

As she headed for the driving range, she stopped to pick up a bucket of balls at the pro shop.

"Hear about our new chef?" Karl asked. Karl had been the pro here as long as Molly could remember. "He's straight from Paris. Makes a heck of a Crème Brule."

"Just what I'll need after whacking this bucket of balls," replied Molly.

She picked up the bucket, pushed open the door, and walked over to the putting green. "No sense in starting off with the strenuous stuff. I'll just warm up a little with some putting." After trying some short putts, some long putts and some near misses, she decided to give the driving range a try. Not too many people were on it today, so she had plenty of choices. She strode up to the nearest spot, placed her ball on the rubber tee, took her stance, kept her head down and her eye on the ball. Slowly she moved the club head on the back swing keeping her elbow straight. "Nice and easy!" she thought to herself as she swung the club forward. With a resounding crack the club met the ball and the ball sailed out into the grass about 75 yards. "Not bad for an old lady," she thought. She teed up the next ball and continued to hit balls for another twenty minutes. A few of them even went straight.

"I remember the old adage," she thought. "Hit a ball to the left it's a hook, hit it to the right it's a slice, hit it down the middle it's a miracle. How true."

She returned her empty bucket to the pro shop, put her clubs back in the trunk of her car, and went into the clubhouse to freshen up before lunch.

"A little hair combing, some fresh lipstick, and I'll be ready to meet the world," she thought as she glanced at her reflection in the mirror. "Or maybe a lot of haircombing. Gotta look my best if I'm going to meet this new chef I've been hearing so much about."

She walked into the dining room looking around to see if Angie were there yet. She loved what they had done to the dining room. The dark green carpet matched the paint on the walls exactly. With the new oak tables and chairs and the crisp white curtains at the wide expanse of windows overlooking the course, the whole place looked so inviting. She chose a table near the windows. She had just seated herself when Betty Thompson stopped by her table.

"Hi, Mrs. Donner. Could I get you anything to drink?"

"Yes, Betty. I think I'll have a nice tall glass of lemonade with lots of ice. I'm really thirsty from all the exercise I've had this morning."

"Are you eating alone, or are you expecting someone?" Betty asked.

"Angie O'Connor is meeting me. She should be along any minute." Molly replied.

"I'll be right back with the lemonade. In the meantime you might want to glance over our new menu. We have lots of yummy stuff since Jean-Claude took over. He's the new chef you know."

"Yes, I've heard so many good things about him. How is he to work with?"

"Oh, just fine, as long as you do EVERYTHING his way," said Betty.

As Betty walked away, Molly spied Angie coming into the dining room. Waving her hand to attract Angie's attention, she stopped herself from hollering "Yoo Hoo." "What would Jean-Claude think of that?" she wondered.

"Hi," said Angie as she slid into the chair opposite Molly. "Have you ordered yet?"

"No, but Betty left us a couple new menus. The chilled grilled shrimp salad sounds good to me."

"After looking over the menu for a few minutes, they motioned for Betty to come and take their orders.

"I'll have the shrimp salad," said Molly. "Does that come with those yummy cheesy biscuits?"

"Yes," replied Betty. "I love those don't you?"

"M-m-m. Yes I do," said Angie. "I'll take a couple of those and a bowl of onion soup with a small Caesar salad."

"What would you like to drink, Mrs. O'Connor?"

"I'll have iced tea – no lemon please."

"OK," said Betty. "I'll be right back with the tea and a refill on your lemonade, Mrs. Donner."

"Has the new chef come out yet?" asked Angie. "I heard that sometimes he circulates through the dining room and talks with the guests."

"Haven't seen hide nor hair of him," said Molly. "But, he sure has been the topic of conversation here in Bridgeville. Just to change the subject for a minute, have you seen Beth today? I was supposed to pick up the bazaar money from her today. She said she had wrappers at her house that they use down at the store and she would count the money and wrap the coins, but she had such a busy schedule today that she couldn't make it to the bank. I told her that I'd be glad to make the deposit. I've stopped there a couple times this morning and she hasn't been there either time."

"She said she was having her hair done at Jenny's early today so that she could come out and play a few holes before the game tomorrow. Maybe her hair took longer than she planned. She said she was trying something really different for her."

"Maybe so," said Molly. "I guess I'll stop once more on my way home."

Betty brought their food, Angie's iced tea, and a pitcher of lemonade for Molly. They ate their lunch chatting about the Tuesday bridge game and the up coming golf tournament. Betty stopped to see if they wanted nutty fudge brownies alamode or a slice of cheesecake smothered in cherries for dessert. "I think I'll pass," said Angie. "But is Jean-Claude coming out into the dining room today?"

"No, he left right after getting the lunch specials started. Said he had some shopping to do for dinner. Lamb chops, parslied potatoes, and lemon soufflé for dessert are the specials for tonight and he always likes everything fresh," replied Betty.

"Well, if we can't see the man of the hour, we might as well leave," pouted Angie. She always liked to be the first to meet newcomers to the community just in case they might be looking for a house.

When they finished, they paid their checks and headed for their cars. As they left the clubhouse, they met Alice Clark and Connie Ryan coming through the door.

"Checking out the competition?" Angie asked Connie.

"Oh yes," said Connie. You always have to know what's going on in the food business."

Angie and Molly walked on to the parking lot, got into their cars, and pulled out onto River Road – Molly going to Beth's and Angie heading back to the office.

CHEESE GARLIC BISCUITS
(AKA RED LOBSTER BISCUITS)

2 c. Bisquick
2/3 c. milk
1/2 c. grated cheddar cheese
1/2 c. melted butter
1/4 tsp. garlic salt

Mix Bisquick, milk and cheddar until a soft ball forms.

Beat vigorously for 30 seconds.

Drop by balls onto an ungreased baking sheet and bake at 450 degrees for 8 to 10 minutes.

Mix butter and garlic and brush on rolls while still on the pan and hot.

Printed from **COOKS.COM**

Chapter 14

Molly drove into her driveway pressing the button on her garage door opener. "Three strikes and you're out," she thought. "I don't know what happened to you, Beth, but I'm not going back to your house again today. I'll just call you later and make arrangements to pick up the money tomorrow."

She changed into her grubbies and went into the potting shed Seth had built for her behind the garage. Taking a tray down from the shelf, she placed twelve one-inch green plastic pots on it. She plunged her trowel into a new bag of potting soil and scooped out some of the dark black dirt. She put a shovel full into each pot and mixed in a little vermiculite. Then she cut a slip off the geraniums that were planted in the hanging baskets on her front porch. She carefully dipped the cut end of the plant into some rooting compound, punched a hole in the soil in the first pot, and slid the stem down into the hole. She patted the soil around the stem and started cutting another slip. She loved feeling the dirt on her hands, the smell of the cuttings, and the knowledge that next summer she'd have lots of lovely red flowers in pots on the patio, in the gazebo, and on the front porch. She finished cutting the plants she had in the potting shed, picked up the shovel and went out to dig up the plants growing in the bed down by the dock. As she dug in the soft earth, she thought to herself, "I've got to plant those daffodil and crocus bulbs that I bought in St. Louis the last time I went down to visit Kate."

Flowers had literally saved her life especially after that awful July day eleven years ago when she received the call from the hospital that Seth had been in an accident coming home from a coaches clinic in Springfield. By the time she got to the hospital, he was dead from injuries received in a head-on collision with a drunk driver. She was stunned. Nora found her sitting in the same chair she had been sitting in when the doctor gave her the news. Slowly Nora got her to move toward the car, drove her home, and called her children.

Ken, Sandy, and their one-year old son, Tim, came down from Western Springs and Kate and Doug came up from St. Louis. They made it through the next few days of funeral plans, visitations, and finally the funeral itself. After everyone went home, Molly immersed herself in gardening – digging, planting, transplanting, pruning, fertilizing, weeding, mowing, mulching. She worked so hard physically that she would flop into bed at the end of the day and drop into a deep, dreamless sleep. Family and friends called and stopped by to see how she was doing. Their endless goodwill and countless meals helped her survive the terrible loss. As August marched relentlessly on toward Labor Day and the beginning of school, Molly realized that she just couldn't go back. She called Brian O'Connor and asked if she could meet with him. On a Tuesday afternoon, she walked into the high school past the trophy cases so filled with memories for her both from the times Seth had played on winning teams and the times when he had coached them. She sat down in Brian's office trying to compose herself but was too overcome to talk. Brian left her alone for a few minutes while he went to get two cups of coffee. By the time he got back, she was herself again and could discuss her plan to retire. He reluctantly agreed that 30 years was long enough to teach and that he would post her job. They would hire another teacher, but she would never be replaced.

Two weeks later, Molly got a phone call from Nora reminding her that the Tuesday Bridge Club was having its first get-together on Tuesday at Jenny's apartment.

After four hands, Molly and Peggy Fitch chatted while they waited to change tables. Molly talked about her gardening and Peggy, a former Art teacher at the high school, talked about her ceramic pots. The shed behind her house was filled with projects her former students had left unclaimed and others she had made herself. Her husband was threatening to throw some of them out if she insisted on making more. She just couldn't bring herself to part with them. Nora suggested that they get together and open a flower shop putting Molly's plants into Peggy's pots. Everyone laughed and changed tables to play the next hand. Nora's plan was all but forgotten.

Right before Thanksgiving Ken decided to quit his job in the Chicago area and accept the position of Assistant Police Chief in Bridgeville. He and Sandy moved in with Molly while they looked for a house. Thanksgiving dinner was a lot of fun especially with Tim who was walking and talking by now. The next day Sandy and Angie O'Connor looked for a house while Grandma Molly babysat. They finally found a cute little cape cod just down the street from Nora and only a few blocks from the police station. It had a big yard surrounded by a white picket fence so they did not have to worry about Tim running out into the street. By Christmas they had finished painting and wallpapering and were ready to have Christmas dinner in their new dining room. Sandy baked the ham and the hot rolls, Kate brought peas and water chestnuts in a cream sauce and a molded jello salad, and Molly brought sweet potato casserole complete with pecans and marshmallows and a variety of their favorite Christmas cookies.

In February, the Tuesday Bridge Club met at Peggy Fitch's. Molly was the first to arrive so Peggy took her out to the shed to show her the pots she had accumulated. As they looked over the brightly colored array, they talked again about the possibility of starting a flower shop. Molly had some money from Seth's estate that she could use to rent the shop. Peggy had some money from retirement that she could chip in on inventory. They decided to start off with potted, growing plants at first. That way they would not have to invest in a cooler for cut flowers.

They found a shop downtown that used to be a bakery. The easy part was cleaning and painting. Coming up with a name was a challenge. Peggy and Molly's Flower Shop was the obvious choice but not too appealing. They also considered Plants and Pots, The Green Thumb, Bridgeville Flowers and several others. Finally, after polling their friends, they settled on Petals and Pots. They painted the floor a bright blue. The walls were mustard yellow with two bright blue stripes running around the room shoulder high. They painted two old stepladders red and put dark green planks across the rungs to hold the potted plants. In the storeroom they found an old baker's rack which they painted purple. Pushing it up against the wall opposite the stepladders, they placed more pots on its shelves. The counter was painted apple green and dangling down from the ceiling were several pots in macramé chords. Stripping the black paint off the old tin ceiling was too much of a job for Molly and Peggy, so they hired a professional to return it to its original brass finish. By the first of April, they were ready to open for business.

By 3:00 on the first day, they were completely sold out. They put a sign in the window – Gone Fishin' – and went out to Molly's to pot more plants. They called Sandy to see if she could help. Since school was out for the day, she left Tim with the high school girl next door and headed out to Molly's. They had a great afternoon filling pots with dirt and transporting them back to town. They realized that day that they were going to have to do most of their work in the back room of the shop and stop running out to Molly's. It took too much time and gas. They also realized that they were going to need help. After talking it over with Ken, Sandy agreed to work three days a week in the shop. Peggy decided she, too, needed help making pots and contacted one of her former students, Rosie Gilmore, who was delighted to earn money doing something she loved. The four of them worked well together for several years. Soon Peggy and Molly wanted to limit their involvement. They hired two new girls and slowly worked themselves out of a job. The year that Ken was named Chief of Police, Sandy and Rosie bought the shop. Molly was relieved to have time to tend the flowers around her house and Peggy was relieved to have time to travel with her husband.

"Stop reminiscing!" Molly thought. She put the dug up plants on the counter in the potting shed, leaned the spade against the wall at the end of the workbench and went inside to clean up. She walked through the garage and into the laundry room where she washed her hands. In the kitchen she poured herself a Pepsi with lots of ice, and plopped down in the family room to watch "Murder She Wrote" on tv. She pulled the afghan over her feet and soon she was sound asleep. When she woke up, the ice in the Pepsi had melted and "Magnum PI" was blaring away.

She hastily got up from the chair thinking, "What would people think if they saw me sleeping in the middle of the afternoon?"

After putting a load of towels in the washer, she looked through the refrigerator trying to decide what to have for supper.

"I had so much for lunch that I should skip supper," she thought. "Maybe just a salad. No. I had salad for lunch. Oh, there's cold roast beef left over from Sunday dinner. I think I'll have a roast beef sandwich with a slice of tomato and one of those pears I got the other day at the Farmer's Market. They were hard as a rock when I brought them home, but they've been in that brown paper sack on the counter for three days so they should be just right."

She sat down at the table in the kitchen to eat and read the Tribune. After reading about all the tragedy in the world, she relaxed thinking how peaceful it was living in Bridgeville.

Chapter 15

Phinias C. Bartholomew was born on May 7, 1880, in Hamilton, IL, on the banks of the Mississippi River. His mother and he lived in a house next door to the fire station where she took in washing for the townspeople in order to make ends meet. It was a quiet life until the sternwheelers docked. As a young boy Phinias would hear their whistles blow and knew it wouldn't be long before his father would come roaring in the door and the fun would begin.

Conrad Bartholomew was a riverboat gambler who earned his living playing poker up and down the Mississippi from Galena to New Orleans. He loved life. He loved people. But most of all, he loved poker.

When he was in Hamilton, life was a lot more fun at the Bartholomew house. The piano in the parlor came to life as he ran his fingers over the keyboard thumping out the favorite tunes of the day. Phinias and his mother would sing and dance around the house as his father tickled the ivories. They had steak every night. Sometimes the neighbors came over and they rolled up the carpet and danced. Two weeks later the boat would stop on its return trip down the river and Conrad would pack his grip. Phinias and he walked to the pier hand in hand talking a blue streak, trying to get in all the conversation they could before the boat sailed.

One June day when Phinias was about five years old, Conrad put down his suitcase as they reached the pier and handed Phinias a deck of cards. Taking another deck out of his pocket he proceeded to show Phinias a card trick.

"Teach me how to do that!" Phinias shouted.

"OK," said his dad. After several tries, Phinias heard his dad say, "You practice that while I'm gone and when I get back I'll show you another."

With that he gave Phinias a hug, picked up his suitcase, swung up the gangplank, and disappeared into the ship. Phinias stood on the dock waving at the boat as it slowly disappeared into the distance. He practiced and practiced his card trick. By the time his father returned, he could do it so smoothly that his dad was impressed. True to his word, he taught Phinias another trick. Each time he came home, they would spend time together working on more and more manipulations of the cards. By the time he was 12 years old, Phinias could palm an ace and deal off the bottom as well as his dad could. He spent hours practicing in the old shed out behind the house because his mother would not have approved had she known.

When he was 13, he snuck into the saloon and watched the poker game going on. Week after week he would watch them play. The big complaint was the poor quality of the cards. After being shuffled several times, the cardboard would start to bend. Soon the players needed a new deck. What they needed was cards that lasted longer. That gave Phinias an idea. He spent long hours in the shed, but he was no longer practicing card tricks. Now he was working on a better deck of cards.

When he came up with a product, he took it to Silas, the bartender in the saloon, begging him to give his new cards a try. At first Silas was reluctant to take a chance on this rag-tag looking boy. Finally, he relented. The first deck didn't last as long as Phinias had hoped, but he didn't give up. He went back to the shed and tried something else. Another try at the saloon. Another disappointment. But Phinias was relentless. He just kept improving and improving the cards. Finally he had a product that the card players liked. But he couldn't make a living supplying cards to one saloon. He put his products into a knapsack, packed a lunch, and hopped on his bicycle to peddle his cards to towns in the area. His first stop was at Warsaw. He parked his bike in the shade and strolled into the saloon.

"Hi," he said to the bartender. "I'm Phinias Bartholomew and I'm here to sell you some cards that will give you a great deal."

"Phinias?" said the bartender. "What kind of a name is that? I'm just going to call you Bart, OK?"

"Bart it is," said Phinias who was pleased at having a nickname.

The bartender bought four decks after Phinias did a few card tricks and some fancy shuffling for him. Pocketing the money, he hopped on his bicycle and headed for the next town. He made several sales that day and enough money to buy supplies to make more cards. He and his trusty bicycle ventured farther and farther from Hamilton. His reputation was spreading all along the western part of Illinois from Carthage to Quincy. Soon the cards were selling themselves. One day he walked into the saloon in Hamilton and Silas said to him, "What are you going to call those cards of yours? We've had lots of guys asking for the 'cards that kid on the bicycle sells.' I thought maybe you could call them 'cycle cards.' "

"Great idea," said Bart. "I think I'll put that name on the paper I wrap them in."

Business was booming. His mom was able to stop taking in washing. Life was good. Then the unthinkable happened. His dad was shot by an angry poker player and died on the way back to Hamilton. Bart and his mother picked up the body and accompanied it to the mortuary. They made arrangements for the funeral. The house seemed very lonely. Even though his dad was gone for weeks at a time, they always knew he'd be home soon and the fun would begin again. Now it was like the light had gone out of their lives.

The years passed. One day Bart's mom received a letter from Milltown. Her maiden aunt had died and left her a house complete with furnishings and even a car. They notified their landlord, packed their few belongings and hired Silas' brother-in-law to move them east to Milltown.

The house was a two-story house on a big lot with a carriage house behind. Part of the carriage house was used as a garage for the aunt's Oldsmobile. There was plenty of room left over for Phinias to set up a shop to produce his cards. Milltown was a whole new market. He set out on his bicycle to sell his cards. Soon he was getting orders from Milltown as well as from the customers he had in the Hamilton area. He started using the car to make the rounds of his customers. It took so much time to get orders and make deliveries that he found it hard to find time to produce the cards.

After a week of 20-hour days, his mother suggested to him that since he was so good at selling, he should hire someone to create the cards. Within two days of taking out an ad in the Milltown Observer he had five applications. He and his mother conducted the interviews at the kitchen table. The third young man was just who they were looking for. He was hired and agreed to start on Monday morning. He was the first of many. The business grew steadily year after year. Bart finally had to move into larger quarters. Across the river on the outskirts of the village of Bridgeville, Bart found a large building that was perfect for his needs. He bought it and moved his entire operation there in 1900.

In 1901, he married Pollyanna Bathgate. They lived with his mother while they saved enough money to build their dream house on the five acres adjoining the property where his card factory was located. He contacted a young architect named Frank Lloyd Wright to design the house. It was a lovely sight to behold with its sweeping lines and view from the many rooms facing the river. Bart and Pollyanna moved in on April 18, 1902, and lived there until their deaths raising their only daughter, Abby, among the apple orchards and gardens.

Bart hired and fired many men in his life, but his favorite employee was a red-headed, firey tempered young man named Sean Magee. He was hard working, fun loving, and full of good ideas about how to run the Cycle Card Company. When Bart died, his will named his daughter CEO of the company but made Sean the President in charge of the day-to-day operations.

Several years after taking over the reins of the company, Sean came up with a plan to have an annual bridge tournament in Bridgeville. The top prize was to be $1,000 with $500 for the second prize. The entry fee would be $2.00 per couple and he would advertise in the Chicago, St. Louis, Cleveland, Indianapolis, and Detroit newspapers as well as hang posters on telephone poles in cities throughout the state of Illinois.

The first tournament took place in 1936 on the third weekend in October. Two hundred and fifty-six advance registrations came pouring in after the newspapers ran the advertisements. Sean formed a committee of people from the community to deal with room reservations, food, transportation, and most importantly the logistics of tournament play. They had arranged with the school board to hold the tournament at the high school. The desks were moved to the side of the room after school was out at 3:00 on Friday and two card tables were placed in the Math room, English rooms, history room, geography room, French room, and the Home Ec. room. Fourteen tables were set up in the Study Hall and six on the stage in the auditorium. Sixteen tables were set up in the gym and fourteen more in the cafeteria.

As people registered, they were sent a bag of goodies from the town – a small box of fudge from the Sugar Plum, a box of bath salts from the Emporium, a scented candle from the Antique Shoppe, and of course a deck of Cycle Cards. Also included in the bag were tickets with their tournament entry number on them. The playoff brackets were posted on bulletin boards around the school. It was to be a single elimination contest. The losers were invited to stay and play party bridge with other losers if they liked. The whole town was adorned with red, white, and blue bunting which added to the festive air.

Participants were encouraged to make their room reservations early. After the Blue Bottle Inn, The Bridgeville Hotel, the Ladner Brothers Hotel, and the River Bend Hotel were full, people started making reservations in Milltown. The old Quaker Oats grain elevator had been converted by Peter Palmer of Chicago into a very unusual hotel. Diamond-tipped saws had been used to saw large openings in the twelve-inch thick concrete walls. All the rooms were round with French doors opening off the rooms onto balconies overlooking the river to the West or the beautifully landscaped grounds in the other directions. A small creek flowed through those grounds with bridges spanning its many twists and turns. Flowerbeds of marigolds, snapdragons, petunias, pansies and zinnias grew profusely along the paths with benches placed here and there for guests to sit and rest beneath giant oak trees. It was peaceful and serene after the cut-throat atmosphere of the tournament.

The hotel dining rooms and the Mayflower Restaurant were about the only places to eat in town. To ease the frustration of standing in long lines, churches began serving lunches and dinners. The Ladies Aid at the Baptist and Presbyterian Churches and the Alter Society at the Catholic Church got together and decided they would coordinate their meals so that they all served the same thing. That way everyone would be fed and there wouldn't be competition to see who could outdo whom. Fish, cottage fries, and coleslaw would be the fare on Friday night, sandwiches, potato salad, and lemonade would be served for Saturday lunch, Swiss Steak, green beans, and mashed potatoes would be offered on Saturday night, and pork chops, scalloped potatoes, and stewed tomatoes would be served on Sunday for lunch. Homemade pies, cookies, and cupcakes were offered as dessert with every meal. As the commercial places to stay filled up, many people opened their homes to one or two couples. Friendships were made as tournament players returned year after year. Win or lose, everyone had a good time.

The tournament began at 7:00 on Friday evening. By 9:30, 128 teams had been eliminated. Saturday morning, play began at 8:00 a.m. for the remaining 128 teams. Losers were often found wandering the streets of Bridgeville, shopping in the Antique Shoppe or the Emporium, stopping for ice cream at the Apothecary and Sundries Shop, or strolling up and down the tree lined streets admiring the Victorian homes.

After two rounds of play on Saturday morning, the combatants broke for lunch. Thirty-two teams resumed play at 1:30. By 9:00 on Saturday evening, four teams remained. The Saturday evening and Sunday afternoon games were played in the gym. Many people sat in the bleachers quietly watching the play. Others attended the high school band concert at the pavilion in the park or went to the play in the Auditorium put on by the High School Thespian Club. Some took advantage of the empty classrooms to play bridge with new acquaintances they had met at the tournament. The final game began at 2:30 Sunday afternoon with the prizes being awarded at the completion of that game.

As the years went by, the tournament grew and grew. People came from as far away as California and New York. More and more residents opened their homes to players and activities such as antique auto shows, rock concerts, swing bands, and bingo were added. Some people brought campers and grilled outside. The smell of charcoal filled the autumn air.

Soon the tournament outgrew the High School. Sean oversaw the building of a Community Center on River Road near the park. It was large enough to house all the tournament play and used for community activities throughout the rest of the year. Built out of concrete block, it was serviceable but not very attractive. Even painting it did not help its appearance. Soon the building became affectionately known as BUB (Big Ugly Building) by the locals.

The first year of the tournament was a great year for Sean Magee – President of a company he loved and a new daughter named Molly to join her brothers Patrick and Casey.

Abby Bartholomew lived in her parents' house all of her days. Her frail nature kept her inside most of the time, but occasionally people crossing the bridge to Milltown would see her walking in her garden in the cool of a summer evening. Many times her nurse or her gardener would be walking with her. In 1950, about 15 years after her father's death, Abby died of a heart attack. With no one to inherit the house, it stood empty for years. The Cycle Card Company maintained it thinking that one day they would open it as a museum like the Robie house that Frank Lloyd Wright had built in Chicago.

In 1967, Sean Magee retired. The new President thought the maintenance of the Bartholomew House was too big an expense, so he sold it to Arnold Graham who turned it into a hotel. For 16 years the house steadily declined until Pete and Connie Ryan rescued it in 1983 and turned it into The Four Aces Restaurant.

Chapter 16

Pete Ryan grew up in Evansville, Illinois. At 5' 10" he was the tallest boy in his Freshman class. He continued to grow all through high school. As a Senior he was pushing 6' 5". The girls loved his brown hair and his laughing blue eyes that twinkled as though he had just heard a great joke. The boys liked his easy going ways off the field and his fierce competitiveness when he was on their team. He enrolled at the University of Illinois where he majored in Hotel and Restaurant Management and pledged Sigma Alpha Epsilon fraternity. He ate his meals at the Kappa Kappa Gamma sorority house where he worked as a waiter. One morning at the beginning of his Sophomore year, as he was mopping the kitchen floor for his buddy who had a test, Connie Kelly came in for a cup of coffee. She sat on a stool in the corner of the kitchen drinking her coffee and talking to Pete as he worked.

"Don't I know you from somewhere?" she asked.

"Yea. I'm in a lot of your classes," he answered.

"Right," she said. "You always sit way in the back."

"Yea, because that way I can sit with my legs out in the aisle and not trip anyone. That's the curse of being tall – dealing with long legs that is."

They continued to talk on a daily basis. Briefly of course because it was against house rules for the girls to fraternize with the waiters. After several weeks of walking home after class together, sneaking out for a coke, and once arranging to meet at the movies where they held hands in the dark before leaving separately, Pete asked Connie if she'd like to go see Peter, Paul, and Mary with him when they came to campus.

"I'm sorry," she said. "I already have a date."

"How 'bout doing something on Sunday then?" he asked.

"I'd love to, but what about our house rules? I don't want you to lose your job."

"I can't lose what I don't have anymore. I'm quitting today and starting at the Chi Omega house on Monday. I just can't stand seeing you everyday and not being able to date you."

Connie and Pete went to Kickapoo Lake on Sunday. It was a wonderful day and on the way home he asked her if she'd wear his pin. Beaming from ear to ear, she said, "Yes." They spent most of everyday together from then until Christmas. During the holiday season, they visited each others families. For Christmas, Pete gave Connie a diamond and they were married on Valentine's Day. They moved into a small apartment on Green Street which was walking distance to classes and work. Pete went to work at the new Holiday Inn out by the expressway and Connie worked at the Student Union in the faculty cafeteria. They both loved food and took turns fixing dinner, each trying to outdo the other by creating new, unusual, and inexpensive dishes on their shoestring budget. They dreamed of the day when they would graduate and have a restaurant of their own.

During Pete's Senior year, he had an internship at George Diamond's restaurant in Chicago. He lived with Connie's parents in Arlington Heights for ten weeks while Connie stayed in their apartment in Champaign. She was one of the lucky few who was assigned an internship in Urbana at the Lincoln Hotel. Not only was it good training, but she did not have to leave campus to do it.

Two weeks before graduation day, Pete got a job offer from Phil Smit's restaurant in Chicago Heights. The salary was excellent, the job sounded interesting, and there was the prospect of a job for Connie opening up in October. They packed their few belongings and found an apartment in Park Forest.

Connie's job at Phil Smit's never materialized. After two months of waiting, she decided to take some initiative and find a job herself. She was dying to put into practice everything she had learned in college. She found just what she was looking for at the Farmer's Daughter in Orland Park. It was a small, family owned business that was frequented by many of the local people as well as attracting well-known celebrities such as Bob Hope and Phyllis Diller.

It was at the Farmer's Daughter that she met Beth Sheridan. After Steve and Beth moved to Bridgeville, Pete and Connie made several weekend visits. On one of these visits they fell in love with the Bartholomew House. Soon they could think of nothing else. They quit their jobs, cashed in their savings bonds, and bought the dilapidated old house. It took months of remodeling to bring back the former glory. While Pete worked with the carpenters, Connie worked with Peggy Fitch and Molly trying to restore the gardens. Soon it was a showplace of central Illinois. People came from everywhere to admire the architecture of Frank Lloyd Wright and to amble through the beautiful gardens.

Deciding what to serve at the restaurant had been easy. They would have a special everyday. On Sunday they would feature turkey with cornbread stuffing accompanied by Aunt Emma's molded cranberry salad. Meat loaf and baked potatoes on Monday. Pork Chops, scalloped potatoes and homemade applesauce on Tuesday. Chicken Pot Pie and Waldorf salad on Wednesday. Steak and hash browns on Thursday. Fish and Chips on Friday. And roast beef, mashed potatoes and gravy on Saturday. All the vegetables were grown in the garden adjoining the restaurant and hiring Gladys Kleinert as the baker was a brilliant stroke of luck. She made the best cloverleaf dinner rolls anyone could ever remember eating. And her fresh blueberry pie was to die for.

One evening while Connie and Pete sat on the glider on the patio resting from a long day of physical activity and looking out over the grassy slope to the river, they mulled over their choices for a name for the restaurant.

"I know," said Connie. "Since we live in Bridgeville, why not name it something to do with cards?"

"Great idea," said Pete. "How about Double Deuces? That has a nice ring to it."

"Why not The Four Aces? You can't get any better than that."

"The Four Aces it is," agreed Pete.

Chapter 17

Molly warmed up a cup of the morning's coffee in the microwave as she put the supper dishes in the dishwasher. She took the coffee into the family room to enjoy it while she flipped around the channels to see if there was anything good on tv. HBO was showing McLintock again, and she always enjoyed a John Wayne movie. Afterwards, she went upstairs, took a hot shower, and hit the sack. Tomorrow was going to be a big day. Why did they sign up to tee off so early?

Morning came twinkling in through the shear curtains at her bedroom windows. The maple bedroom set she and Seth had bought when they moved into their first house glowed with warmth in the bright sunshine. She turned off the alarm clock, put on her robe and went downstairs for coffee and toast. A piece of rye bread she had last night for supper would taste great toasted. She took the loaf out of the bread drawer, sliced off a big hunk and popped it in the toaster oven (too thick for the toaster) for a few minutes. She poured coffee into a mug, put way too much butter on the toast, and took both out on the three-seasons porch to eat and watch the river roll by.

After breakfast, she put on her blue slacks and her lucky blue and red plaid shirt. She grabbed her red windbreaker on her way out the door, making sure she had her car keys and her purse.

Backing out of the driveway, she had to wait for Ben Grant to pass in his yellow VW bug on his way to work. "Ben's car must be in the shop," she thought. "Emily is the one who usually drives the bug."

She drove along River Road to the golf course and parked her car. As she looked around to see if anyone from her foursome was there yet, she spied a black Probe that looked like Beth's car.

"Is she here already?" wondered Molly. "I thought she said she didn't tee off until later this morning. Maybe she's in the coffee shop. I'll go in and make arrangements with her to pick up that bazaar money later."

But when she got to the coffee shop, no one was there except Angie who was having coffee and the biggest sweetroll Molly had ever seen.

"Hi," Angie said. "Come and help me eat this sweetroll. I don't know who Jean-Claude is used to feeding, but I think this would feed the entire football team with some left over."

"Oh, I can't eat another thing," replied Molly. "I thought I saw Beth's car in the parking lot and that she might be in here."

"I think that is her car." Said Angie. "It was here when I got here and from the dew that was all over it, I'd say it was here all night."

"How odd," said Molly. "Maybe Steve got back from New York and they both went home in his car. Well, I'll catch up with her later."

Angie paid her bill and the two of them went in to the ladies locker room to put on their golf shoes.

They walked out of the locker room to their cars to get their clubs. Just as Molly was lifting hers from the trunk a cheery voice called out, "Hold it a second, Mrs. D. I believe that's part of my job today." Jimmy Reed came loping across the parking lot toward Molly. He grabbed the clubs and swung them easily from the trunk. "Looks like I got here just in time," he said.

"Oh, Jimmy," said Molly. "I almost forgot about you. Good thing you got here when you did or I would have teed off and gone off without you."

They met Angie, Joan Kendell, and Karen Blake near the first tee. "Boy, are you privileged," said Karen. "I didn't know we were going to have caddies."

"Oh, you're just jealous because you didn't think of it," laughed Molly.

At exactly 8:15 they teed off. As they approached the third tee, the wheel fell off Molly's cart that Jimmy was pulling. "Oh, no!" she moaned. "Now what'll I do?"

"It's nothing," said Jimmy. "Just a loose nut. I'll run back to the club house and get a screwdriver. You ladies go ahead and tee off. I won't be a minute."

Angie hit a beautiful shot straight down the middle of the fairway. Joan's tee shot was also down the middle but not quite as far as Angie's. Karen's shot started out straight but slowly arched to the right and landed in the rough.

"Two down the middle and one to the right," said Molly. "With my luck my shot will go to the left directly into those trees."

She put her ball on the tee, took her stance and, true to her prediction, hit the ball to the left straight into the woods. As she tramped around looking for her ball, she saw a golf cart down by the footbridge that went over the creek.

"I wonder who left their cart out here?" she thought. She bent down to pick up her ball and headed back to the fairway.

"Guess you'll have to take a one stroke penalty," teased Joan as Molly dropped her ball on the course. They played the next six holes and went into the clubhouse for a cold drink. They asked Jimmy to join them, but he said he had to make a phone call first and that he would see them inside.

"I'm going to talk to Karl and report the cart I found," said Molly.

"What cart?" said Angie.

"The cart that is out in the woods near the bridge on number 3. I found it when I went looking for my ball," replied Molly.

"Why didn't you say something before this?" asked Angie.

"I was so upset by having to take a penalty stroke that I forgot all about it until I saw the carts lined up over there by the pro shop," said Molly.

She walked over to the pro shop looking for Karl. He wasn't inside so she walked around to the back and found him talking to a customer who was trying out a new set of clubs. He turned when he heard her golf shoes crunch on the gravel. "Well, hello, Molly," he beamed. "How'd you do this morning?"

"Not too bad considering," said Molly, "but that's not why I'm here. I came to tell you that I found one of your carts over by number 3."

"You did?" he said. "Funny nobody else mentioned it."

"Well, it's back in the woods where the foot bridge crosses the stream."

"I'll walk over there and see what's going on," he said. "Thanks for the tip."

Karl went off toward hole number 3 and Molly went in to join the others in the clubhouse. She motioned to Betty that she was thirsty. Betty delivered the drinks to table six and came over to take Molly's order.

"I'll have a Pepsi," said Molly, "with lots of ice. And I'll have an order of those jalepeno poppers too. Someone told me they were really good here."

"They're delicious," said Betty. "Are you ladies coming back for lunch after playing the back nine?"

"We thought we would," said Angie. "Are they having anything special?"

"Yes, Jean-Claude has outdone himself. He's having a soup, sandwich and salad bar. The soups are lobster bisque, chicken and dumplings, and Texas chili. There will be shaved ham, turkey, roast beef, and corned beef to pile on various kinds of rolls as well as brats on the grill along with potato salad, coleslaw, and pasta salad. It's all going to be laid out on the buffet table set up in the bar. It's really quite a feast," said Betty.

"Sounds good to us," they all said in a chorus.

They finished their snack, rounded up Jimmy from the phone booth, and teed off on number 10. They proceeded to play the back nine without incidence. As they dropped off their clubs and headed in for lunch, Karl called out to Molly. She turned and walked toward him. "You know that cart you saw?" he asked Molly. "It was the one Beth Sheridan took out early yesterday morning. It got so busy later on that I didn't notice that it wasn't returned. I wonder why she left it out there?"

"I don't think she did," said Molly. "I think her car is still in the parking lot. I think she might be hurt and still out there somewhere. We should go out and take a look. I'll get the others and meet you there."

Karl headed toward number 3 and Molly went into the clubhouse to round up the others. They spent a half hour searching for Beth. All they found were some bloody leaves by the bridge.

"I think we should call Ken," said Molly. "Something happened here."

They got in the carts and headed back to the telephone in the pro shop. They got through to the Bridgeville Police Department and asked Bernice to send the chief of police to the golf course. Ken showed up 10 minutes later and strode into the pro shop.

"Hello, Mom," he said to Molly. "What's up?"

"Oh, Ken," said Molly, "we think something dreadful has happened to Beth Sheridan. We found the cart she rented over by number 3 and blood on the leaves near the bridge."

Ken told them to stay there while he looked around. Then he went to his car and called for Dean to bring the dog from the station.

"You ladies might as well go home," said Ken. "I'll let you know if we find anything."

"We'd rather stay," replied Molly.

The dog sniffed the bloody leaves and took off through the woods dragging Dean behind him. They came out of the woods on the service road. The dog sniffed around a little bit and then sat down. They found tire tracks in the soft earth so Ken said to Dean, "Take the dog back to the station and get the plaster cast kit. I'll stay here to make sure we don't have my mother and her friends tromping all over these woods. They've already disturbed it enough."

When Dean returned, they made plaster casts of the tracks and took them to the Goodyear Tire Store on Sheffield Street to see if they could find out what kind of tires made these tracks. Perhaps they could find out what kind of car would have used those tires.

The clerk at the Goodyear store said it would take him some time to make a match. Ken said to Dean, "It just occurred to me that we might be making a mountain out of a molehill. We're not really sure that anything is wrong with Beth. That blood may be from something totally different. Maybe we should go over to her house and see if she's there. I'll bet she has some logical explanation about why she didn't return the cart."

As Ken and Dean pulled into the alley behind Sheridan's house, a dark blue Suburban pulled up behind them and Steve Sheridan stepped out.

Chapter 18

Steve Sheridan was a tall, blond, broad shouldered athletic man who looked so good in the clothes he wore that he was a walking advertisement for the clothing he and Beth sold in their store, the Plush Pony.

Steve grew up in Calumet City, Illinois. His dad worked in a steel mill in Gary, Indiana, but since his wife died when Steve was little, Chuck spent all his spare time with Steve teaching him to bat, throw, run, block, and tackle. By the time Steve was in high school, he was the starting split end on the football team. He was scouted by major universities: Illinois, Michigan, Northwestern being just a few. He chose Illinois because his best friend was going to school there. Al and Steve had lived in the same neighborhood all their lives. They had competed on the athletic fields and in the classroom all through school. So it was inevitable that they would both attend the same college. Although Steve was red-shirted his Freshman year, he was the starting end his Sophomore year. It was a thrill playing in front of 60,000 cheering fans. The Fighting Illini had a great team that year. They rolled over Perdue, Indiana, Michigan State, and Iowa. By the fifth game of the season, everyone in the stands was yelling, "Rose Bowl, Rose Bowl" as the team ran out on the field. The first half went well. He caught three passes, one for a touchdown. They were beating

Ohio State 18-3 at the end of the first half. Ohio State kicked off to Illinois to start the second half. Al caught the ball and returned it to the 40-yard line. Illinois lined up and snapped the ball. The quarterback dropped back five steps and let fly with a 30-yard bomb. Steve who was racing along the sideline stretched to catch the ball that was floating just above his head. As he came down with the ball, an Ohio State safety took a flying leap hitting Steve just above the knee. There was a sickening snap and Steve fell to the ground grabbing his left leg. The trainer ran out on the field, took one look at Steve's leg, and motioned for the stretcher. As they were loading him in the ambulance, Illinois players and Ohio State players alike came over to the sideline to wish him well. Compound fracture of the femur. That was the diagnosis. Six weeks in a cast and then weeks of therapy to get his leg back in shape. He hobbled around the campus, slipping and sliding on crutches finishing the semester exams and heading home for term break. During the break he talked to his doctor about the chances of his playing football again. The doctor was not optimistic. He explained that when the bone broke, it came through the muscle and skin which damaged the muscle so much that it would take longer than six months to rehabilitate.

After lots of soul searching, Steve decided to drop out of school, get a job, and work really hard to get his leg back in shape. The kinds of jobs he could do with a cast on were limited. He tried frying hamburgers at the neighborhood McDonald's, but he couldn't stand for eight hours. After two days there he quit and tried working as a janitor for St. Mary's church. But he didn't like janitorial work. Before the week was over he was searching the want ads looking for another job.

On Saturday he spied an ad in the <u>Sun Times</u> for a salesman in the Men's Department at Marshall Field's. He'd never considered selling clothes before but thought it was something he could do. After typing up his resume and a letter of application, he decided to take it in personally rather than mail it. He put on the suit his dad had bought him for high school graduation and headed for the main store at State and Madison.

The personnel department was so impressed with him that they sent him up to the Men's Department to talk with Mr. Granger, the manager. The next day he began a job that would change his life. He was hard working, friendly, and a great salesman. Soon men were asking for him when they shopped at Field's. After a few weeks he got a promotion. By the end of March he was the third highest salesman in the department. Mr. Granger took such a liking to the young man that he started grooming him to become department head someday. They went on buying trips to New York, Paris, and Rome. Steve even spent several weeks in Paris visiting haut courtier and learning about men's fashions. The more he learned, the more the wanted to learn.

The Thursday before Memorial Day, he had just returned to Chicago from one such buying trip and was eating lunch in the employees' cafeteria on the 13th floor watching the sailboats skid around Lake Michigan. From the corner of his eye, he saw a cute girl enter the room carrying her tray and looking around shyly for a place to sit. Most of the tables were occupied so he motioned for her to join him. She sat down and introduced herself as Beth Wentworth and said that she was working for the summer in the women's clothing department. They chatted while they ate finding out that they had lots in common: both liked to participate in sports, both were active in church youth groups, and both were living with their parents. The time passed so quickly that they couldn't believe it when it was time to go back to work. They met again after work, talked for a few minutes, and left to catch their trains – he to Calumet City; she to Evanston.

Friday at lunch they met again and decided to go out that night. She gave him directions to her parents' home and they parted agreeing to see each other again at 7:00. What fun! Dinner and a movie had never been so enjoyable. They went out again on Saturday. On Sunday they went to the Museum of Science of Industry. Monday was Memorial Day and they took a picnic lunch to the forest preserves near Orland Park. The hiked, ate, ran, laughed, talked. By the end of the day they were hopelessly in love.

The summer raced by. Before they knew it Labor Day was upon them and Beth was getting ready to go back to school. It wasn't much of a trip since she went to Northwestern. Steve's doctor would not sign a release allowing Steve to play football that fall, so he decided to keep his job at Field's. They talked on the phone every day. She came home every weekend. Thanksgiving vacation was tough. The Friday after Thanksgiving is the biggest shopping day of the year so Steve was tied up all day. Saturday was a repeat of Friday, but Steve had Sunday off and they went to Grant Park and walked along the Lake Michigan shoreline with their coat collars turned up against the wind. It was that day that they talked about getting married.

Right before Christmas, Steve was re-assigned to the Orland Park store as head of the men's department. It was a great promotion with a huge raise and a bonus which he used to buy Beth a diamond ring for Christmas. Both families were thrilled. Somehow they got through the next semester and they were married in June. They bought a 100-year-old Victorian house in the older section of Orland Park just a block from downtown with its antique shops, pharmacy, and the Methodist Church. The house needed some work, but a new coat of paint, some work on the hardwood floors, and a new bathroom put in upstairs next to the master bedroom made the house in move-in shape. Beth spent a wonderful summer shopping for furniture. She found several antique shops in Frankfort, Tinley Park, and Palos Hills. On her rounds she always stopped in Palos Park at the Plush Pony for a rum raisin ice-cream cone. She was originally drawn to this quaint place by the full-sized carousel pony covered with dark red plush material in the window. At first she thought it was another antique shop. But when she stepped inside, she was surrounded by nostalgia. The old-fashioned soda fountain had stools at the counter and little marble topped tables surrounded by chairs with bent wire backs. Even the little old lady who owned the Plush Pony seemed to step out of a picture of by-gone days.

Beth and Mrs. Symington became fast friends. Beth loved to sit and drink a lime phosphate and listen to the stories of early Palos Park. When Mrs. Symington died, her heirs sold the ice cream shop and Beth bought the pony at the auction. She and Steve dragged it up into the attic of the carriage house they used as their garage and covered it lovingly with an old quilt to keep it safe.

Beth finished her Senior year at Northwestern driving from Orland Park to Evanston everyday. For graduation, Beth's parents gave them a trip to Hawaii. When they got back Beth got a job selling women's clothing in a little shop next door to the pharmacy just a block from their house. She and Steve loved the village. They talked about moving farther out of the city and starting a clothing store in a small town.

Beth's father, a first vice-president at Bank One in Chicago, had met Arthur Beck at a bankers' convention in New Orleans. They had a lot in common and had remained friends over the years. Art was the president of the National Bank of Bridgeville. When he heard about Steve and Beth's plans, he suggested that they come to Bridgeville for the weekend, look around, and maybe consider moving there.

He and his wife, Nora, had plenty of room and would love to have the Sheridans stay at their house.

The weekend arrived and Steve and Beth drove south on Route 45 to Bridgeville. Art and Nora had a few people over for dinner on Saturday night to meet them. Sunday morning they went to church and then to the golf course for brunch. After brunch, they drove around the downtown district looking for an empty shop. There was one on Bridge Street just down the street from the movie theater and next door to the confectionery, The Sugar Plum.

When they got back to Beck's, they called Angie O'Connor, the realtor whose sign they had seen in the window of the vacant shop. She was at home and agreed to meet them at the shop. It was just what they were looking for. The bay window would be perfect for the plush pony that lived in the attic of their carriage house. They went back to the real estate office and made an offer, stopped to say goodby to the Becks, and headed for home. Within a week, they had heard from Angie that their offer on the shop was accepted. They gave their two-week notices at work and put their house in Orland Park up for sale.

Three weeks later they closed on the shop, picked up Angie O'Conner, and went to look for a house in Bridgeville. They found one on Polk Street that looked very similar to their house in Orland Park. Only one problem -- the house wasn't for sale. They asked Angie to find out if the owners might be interested in selling. Sure enough. The Daileys told Angie that they had been thinking about moving into the new apartments going up in Milltown and would consider an offer from the Sheridans.

Steve and Beth went back to Orland Park to begin the process of packing up and moving. On moving day, Steve's dad drove the u-haul truck and Steve and Beth each drove a car filled to the brim with stuff. They got settled in and then started in on the shop. The grand opening was a success. Everyone was anxious to see what the new store with the carasoul horse in the window had to offer. They were off and running. They never looked back. Life in Bridgeville was wonderful. They joined the church and the country club. They became involved in the Jay Cees and the community theater. Steve ran for City Council and Angie O'Connor asked Beth to join the Tuesday Bridge Club. The only flaw in their lives was that they had no children. Try as they might, the years rolled by with no hope of a child. They started meeting with the Cradle adoption agency in Chicago hoping that at last they could fill up the many rooms in their large Victorian house on Polk Street.

Even though he was tall and blond and she was short and dark, they were soul mates. No two people ever got along better. Sometimes one would start a sentence and the other would finish it. They had the same taste in music, food, and merchandise for the store. At the end of the day, they would sit over coffee in their big kitchen discussing the events of the day and planning for tomorrow.

Chapter 19

Molly drove home from the golf course and sat by the phone waiting for Ken to call her with more news. She wanted to go along to Beth's but decided this was Ken's field and that she shouldn't butt in. She jumped when the phone rang about 2:30 even though she was expecting the call.

"Are you sitting down?" Ken asked.

"Oh, no. Bad news," thought Molly.

"Did you find her?" she asked.

"Yes. She was at her house in the dining room," Ken replied.

"Was she," Molly stammered, "was she hurt?"

"Dead," Ken said. "Her house was ransacked. Looks like a burglary."

"But what about the blood at the golf course?" Molly asked.

"Lots of unanswered questions, Mom. We'll have to investigate further. So far we don't even have a murder weapon. I've got to go. I just wanted to fill you in because I knew you'd be anxious. See you later."

Molly put the phone down, sat down in the rocking chair and had a good cry. Finally pulling herself together, she got out her cleaning equipment and started scrubbing her kitchen floor. In times of stress, that old floor had gotten a lot of cleaning. It was such a relief to be busy. She finished the kitchen, laundry room and downstairs bathroom before heading upstairs. As she finished the upstairs bathroom, she heaved a sigh. She put the bucket of cleaning supplies back under the sink in the laundry room, took the towels out of the dryer and went to the family room to fold them. She put a CD on and sat down on the couch. How she loved this room with its warm paneling and soft shades of tan, brown and ecru. It calmed her nerves whenever she felt jangled and right now she felt in need of calming.

She put the folded towels in the linen closet and stopped in the kitchen to heat a can of clam chowder and a chunk of corn bread. She sat down to watch TV while she ate. "Boy this tastes really good," she thought to herself. Then she realized it was the first thing she had eaten since breakfast. She put the empty dishes on the end table next to her chair, pulled the afghan over her feet, and settled down to watch "Friends." She woke up to find the sun shining in her eyes and her body stiff from sleeping all night in the chair. Her mind returned to the events of the day before and she realized that in all the turmoil she had forgotten to pay Jimmy Reed for being her caddy. She'd have to go over to the gas station and pay him this morning. But first a couple eggs sunny side up, toast, and a hot cup of coffee. She was starved. She ate slowly reading the Tribune as she ate. She cleaned up the dishes, retrieved her supper dishes from the family room, changed her clothes and headed for town. She stopped at the bank.

"Fifty dollars should be enough," she thought as she punched her code into the ATM. "I'm sure he could use the money for school."

She drove to the Shell station, parked her car and went in to the office.

"Is Jimmy here?" she asked.

"Nope," said Grady O'Mera, the owner. "He left yesterday afternoon for Chicago."

"He did?" she replied. "I thought he was going to start school next semester."

"He is," Grady said. "He just went up to see his advisor and line up a place to live. Said he'd be back on Saturday for his shift. I'm really gonna miss him around here. He hasn't been working here long, but he's a great worker and always friendly. I'm really gonna miss him. Got his mind set on getting him an education up there in Chicago. Like I say, I'm really gonna miss him around here."

Molly said, "I owed him some money. Guess I'll stop in again on Saturday. Always like to pay my debts."

"Why don't you just put the money in an envelope with his name on it?" asked Grady. "I'll stick it in the cash register and that way he can pick it up when he gets back and you won't have to make another trip."

"Great idea," agreed Molly as she pulled her wallet out of her purse and stuffed the money into the envelope Grady was holding out to her. She jotted Jimmy's name across the front of the envelope and handed it back to Grady.

"Thanks a lot!" she said as she turned and left the station. One more task scratched off her "to do" list.

Chapter 20

Jimmy Reed filled up his car at the Shell station and told Grady to take it out of his next paycheck. He pulled out of the station and headed for Chicago. He just had to get out of town for a while. Beth's murder was the most awful thing that had ever happened in Bridgeville. She was a wonderful lady. He'd been working with her on her golf game - she called him her "personal trainer." Maybe a couple days in Chicago would help him get through this. He'd talk to the counselors at ITT about his classes and look around for an apartment. That should take his mind off Beth.

Chapter 21

As she drove away from the Shell Station, Molly thought, "I'll stop by and see Angie." She parked in front of the real estate office, put a quarter in the meter, and walked in.

"Hi, Brenda," she said. "Is Angie around?"

"No. She's out showing some property. She'll be back in about an hour because she has a closing at the Title Office at 10:30," replied Brenda.

"Thanks," said Molly. "I'll call her later."

She got back in her car and drove over to Nora's. She just had to talk to someone. Nora's car was in the driveway when Molly parked in front of her house. She answered the bell on the second ring.

"Oh, thank goodness you're here. I've been dying to talk to you," said Nora.

They sat in Nora's kitchen drinking coffee and munching on peanut butter cookies. As they looked out the windows into the back yard, they saw Steve Sheridan back out of his garage and drive down the alley toward town.

"Poor Steve," said Molly. "He must be devastated by all this."

"Yes, I talked to him this morning when I took over a casserole for his lunch. He said his dad is coming down tonight after work to spend a few days with him," said Nora.

"When is the funeral going to be?" asked Molly.

"Visitation is going to be tomorrow and Sunday after the coroner performs the autopsy. The funeral is going to be on Monday at 2:00. Do you want to go with Art and me?" asked Nora.

"Yes, I would," replied Molly. "Tell me, Nora, did you see anything unusual at Beth's house that morning?"

"Molly! You know I don't spy on my neighbors," said Nora indignantly.

"I know. I didn't mean to imply you were spying on her. I just see that while we're sitting here, we can see anyone driving in or out, but the garage shields the back yard from view."

"I just don't remember seeing anything," said Nora. "But then I wasn't really looking for anything. After Art left for work, I sat here drinking another cup of coffee and reading the <u>Tribune</u>."

"Well, if you remember anything, call me. Together maybe we can figure this out," said Molly as she put her dishes in the sink and fished around in her purse for her car keys. "Good idea about taking something over to Steve. I think I'll go home and whip up a little something. He and his dad will have to keep up their strength."

As Molly pulled away from the curb she glanced back at Nora who was still standing at the door with a pensive look on her face.

Chapter 22

Jimmy shifted his '55 Chevy into third gear as he accelerated to enter the traffic headed North on I-94. He had completely rebuilt the motor, sanded, patched and painted the body, put in new brakes, and transmission and tuned it up till it purred like a kitten. He got lots of appreciative glances from gray haired drivers as he drove along. "Just seeing this wonderful old car must bring back to them memories of drive-in movies, sock hops, and hamburgers and fries at the local hangout," he thought.

Jimmy kept a sharp eye out for Randolph Street. Driving in Chicago was sure a lot different than driving in Bridgeville. Especially when you got to the loop and cars started coming at you from entrance ramps on the right <u>and</u> the left.

Turning left onto Randolph, he drove west until he saw the sign for ITT. He found a parking place on the first level of the parking garage and walked across the street, through the front doors, and up the stairs to his advisor's office which was located on the second floor. Mr. Rinaldi was a short, pudgy man with black hair combed over the bald spot on top of his head. He had a welcoming smile, a hearty handshake and the kindest brown eyes Jimmy had ever seen.

"Sit down, sit down," Mr. Rinaldi said as he pointed to a soft brown leather chair on the side of his desk which was heaped with papers, file folders, and empty Styrofoam cups that had once held numerous cups of coffee.

"Want a cup of coffee or a can of pop?" he asked.

"Yea. Pop would be nice," replied Jimmy as he sank into the chair indicated.

Mr. Rinaldi signaled for his secretary, Wilma, to bring them each a can of Pepsi and settled into his own chair. Leaning back he smiled at Jimmy and said, "What can I do for you today, Jimmy?"

Jimmy popped the top of his can, and he took a long swig of the ice cold liquid.

"I thought I'd look up some place to live today and while I'm here I thought I'd pay a little more toward my tuition," he replied digging in his pocket for his wallet.

"Whoa," said Mr. Rinaldi. "Don't pay me. When we're done here, I'll take you down to the business office. They take care of all the finances. Let's take a look at your schedule on my computer and I'll run off a copy for you to take home with you."

After several minutes of flipping through screens, Jimmy's schedule miraculously appeared. Clicking the mouse a few more times put the printer in motion and soon Mr. Rinaldi and Jimmy were walking down the hall towards the business office.

"When you're through here, come back upstairs. I'll have Wilma give you a list of places to live that you might want to checkout," said Mr. Rinaldi as he handed Jimmy the printout of his schedule. Then he turned to the woman in the first booth and said, "Gina, this is Jimmy Reed. He'll be joining us next semester and wants to put some money down toward his tuition."

Shaking Jimmy's hand he added, "It was good to see you today. Call me anytime and stop in to see me after you get settled up here."

As he turned to go back to his office, he saw Jimmy pull a wad of money from his pocket and lay it on the counter. "What'd you do?" said Mr. Rinaldi. "Rob a bank?"

"No, sir," said Jimmy. "I've been working real hard at any job I could get and saving my money for quite some time now. This has been a dream for a long time and I'm finally in a position to make it come true."

"Good for you, son," said Mr. Rinaldi. "You're just the kind of student we're looking for. But for heaven's sake. Open a bank account. People have been killed for a lot less cash than you have there."

He turned and walked upstairs as Jimmy gave his attention to the cashier. She had pulled his file while he was talking to Mr. Rinaldi and was ready to make the next entry.

"How much did you want to give me today?" said the cute girl holding his file.

"$1500," replied Jimmy his freckled face turning deep red from his square chin to his strawberry blond hair. Slowly he peeled off the bills and counted them out on the counter painfully aware of his rough hands with nicks and cuts on them and ground in grease that he'd been unable to scrub off no matter how hard he tried.

"What nice hands you have," said Gina. "They look like they could fix anything. My dad has hands like that," she said with a smile.

"Thanks, I guess. I mean, thanks," he mumbled as he backed away from the counter.

"Wait," she said. "I've got to give you a receipt."

He stood on one foot and then the other as she counted the money, made the computer entry, and printed out the receipt. As she handed him the slip of paper, she said, "Hang on to that. It'll prove that you've made a payment. It's good to keep them in case our computers crash. They never have, thank goodness, but you never know."

"Thanks," he said again. "I will. I mean, I won't lose it. I mean, I'll put it in a safe spot." He hurridly folded the receipt and stuck it in his wallet. As he put his wallet back into his pocket, she said to him, "Have you found a place to live yet?"

"No," he said. "I'm on my way back to Mr. Rinaldi's office to get a list of possibilities from Wilma."

"Add this address to the list," she said as she jotted down some numbers on a scrap of paper. "The three guys who live across the hall from me are looking for a roommate. The fourth guy just graduated and is moving out as soon as he gets a job. It's a great place to live and it's close enough to school to walk so you won't waste your money on gas or parking. It has a pool and a nice rec room where we all hang out. Lots of students from here live there, so you'll have plenty in common."

"I don't know," said Jimmy. "A place with a pool sounds too rich for my blood."

"No, really. It's very reasonable. If it weren't, I wouldn't be living there."

"I'll think about it," said Jimmy as he turned to go upstairs. "I don't know why I'm going to get that list," he thought as he started to climb. "I would beg, borrow, or steal just to live across the hall from her. What a great smile she has. Just like Beth's."

Chapter 23

Jimmy pulled out of the parking lot following the map Wilma had given him. He drove by a couple of the places she had marked and decided he'd come back to them if Gina's building didn't work out. Already he was thinking of her as Gina and not as the cashier with the beautiful smile. He walked up to the manager's office and stepped inside. A grandmotherly looking lady sitting at a desk looked up as he entered.

"May I help you?" she asked.

"Are you the manager?" Jimmy asked.

"No, I'm the rental agent. The manager is not here at the moment."

"Well, you're the one I need to talk to, I guess," he said. "I'm looking for a place to rent next semester. Gina at the school told me this was a great place to live."

"Gina should get a referral fee," laughed the rental agent. "She's always sending us someone. Come on. I'll show you around."

After taking the tour and talking about the rent, Jimmy spied a familiar face walking through the door. It belonged to a guy from Milltown whom Jimmy had known when they played basketball against each other in high school. Jumping center against each other you got to know a face pretty well.

"Hey, Allen," said Jimmy. "I didn't know you lived here."

"Yea," said Allen. "I couldn't afford to go to school right out of high school so I saved my money and I'm going now. You'll be surprised how many non-traditional students are enrolled here. That's what I like about it."

"Sounds good to me," replied Jimmy.

"Are you thinking of living here?" asked Allen. "'Cause me and my roommates are looking for a fourth."

"Yea, I am," said Jimmy. "I won't be moving in till next semester, though."

"That's ok. George just graduated and is looking for a job. He'll be sticking around for awhile anyway."

"Great," said Jimmy. "Good to see you again."

"Yea, you too," replied Allen. "Here's my number. Let me know what you decide about the apartment."

Jimmy turned back to the rental agent and asked what he would need to do in order to be put on the waiting list.

"Just fill out this application today. We'll process it and contact your references. Then the month before you move in, we'll contact you. At that time you will need to send in a deposit of first and last month's rent. The last month's rent acts as a security deposit. It's really a nice place to live although we do have rules. You are free to come and go as you like, but no loud music after ll:30 at night because we have so many students here who have to get up and go to class in the morning. The rec room and the pool are available for private parties, but you have to arrange for them a week in advance and there is a charge. Otherwise you personally are welcome to use them any time. That's included in your rent. Some of the renters share the cooking responsibilities with their roommates while others just cook for themselves and clean up their own dishes. You'll have to work that out with the guys you live with."

"OK," said Jimmy standing up to leave.

"Oh, wait a minute," said the rental agent. "Don't leave until you've filled out this application."

"Right," said Jimmy. "All that talk about cooking made me hungry. Almost forgot what I came for."

She slid the paper across the desk, handed him a pen and turned to answer the phone while he filled in the blanks. When he finished she was still on the phone, so he just left the form on her desk, waved goodbye to her, and walked back to his car.

Before he pulled away from the curb, he took one more look at the two story, tan brick building. The lawn was neatly mowed. The flowers added to the well-cared for appearance. Yes, his mother would be proud of him. Too bad she hadn't lived to see him get to this stage in his life. Oh well, she must be up in heaven somewhere looking down and smiling at how he had turned out. Or would she? He really was a good boy except for that one small mistake. But nobody knew about that. And now he was on his way to a better life. He could hardly wait.

Chapter 24

Carla Pickins was standing in the office of the Star Dust Motel looking at the list of rooms that needed to be cleaned. She checked the keyboard to see which keys had been turned in already and where she could start her shift.

"Boy," she said to Skip, the desk clerk, "number 5 must've checked out awful early."

"Oh, him," said Skip, pushing his glasses back up from the end of his nose. "He didn't stay very long. Checked in yesterday morning looking like he seen a ghost. Checked out again before noon. Kinda a strange guy if you ask me."

"We have so many strange ones stay here. Why would you remember him?" she asked grabbing a new can of Lysol from the shelf.

"I don't know. He seemed so shook up, I guess. And then he stayed such a short time. Just left his key in his room. I wouldn't even have known he was gone 'cept I seen his truck pulling out of the lot when I went to empty the garbage," he said shrugging his shoulders.

Carla loaded the clean sheets and pillowcases on her cart and headed for number 5. She walked straight to the bathroom carrying her pail of cleaning supplies. After wiping down everything, she replaced the towels even though it looked like only a hand towel had been used and went in to make the bed. As she pulled the rumpled sheets from the bed something fell on the floor at her feet. Skip could hear the screaming clear down at the office. He came running to find Carla staring at the floor. He bent over to pick up the man's windbreaker lying there. It was covered with blood.

"We need to call the police," said Skip as he put his arm around the still shaking girl and guided he toward the office. "But we ain't gonna do it from this room."

Ken arrived about ten minutes later. As Skip described the last person to stay in room 5, Ken wrote down the details in his notebook. Pretty generic: tall – over six feet – nice build, blond hair. No distinguishing characteristics except that he seemed rattled. Skip had noticed that he was driving a dark colored truck, but he had not written down the license plate number. The guy had paid in cash and signed in as John Doe as had the three other John Does ahead of him.

Ken put the jacket into a large plastic evidence bag, placed the bag in the back seat of the police cruiser, and headed for Springfield to the crime lab. As he pulled out on to Route 45, he called Bernice on his radio to tell her of his destination and what time she should expect him back. He also told her to send Dean over to the Star Dust Motel with a fingerprint kit to see if they could find out who left a bloody jacket in room 5.

Chapter 25

Molly stopped at the IGA on her way home from Nora's and picked up the ingredients to make her delicious scalloped potatoes and some hamburger for a meatloaf. Since Chuck Sheridan was going to be staying at Steve's, they'd need some masculine food. Maybe she'd take a nice tossed salad and a chocolate cake for desert. She would put it all in disposable dishes so they would not have to worry about returning anything. They'd probably have lots of meals delivered to them in the next few days by friends and neighbors. Trying to keep all those dishes straight would just add further complications to this topsy-turvy time in their lives. She'd call when she got home to let them know supper was coming.

As she prepared the meal her thoughts constantly went back to Beth's murder. Who could possibly want that sweet young woman killed? What was she doing in the woods so early in the morning? Why was the body moved back to her house? Too many questions and not enough answers.

Molly placed the food in aluminum foil pans stacking them neatly in her picnic basket for easy transporting. She filled a thermos with coffee, put everything on the front seat of her car and drove into town to Steve's house. Steve's dad had arrived that afternoon to help Steve with the funeral arrangements. As Molly stood at the front door, she could see his short, square body rock solid from all the years of working in the steel mill coming down the hallway toward her.

"Hello, Molly," he said as he opened the front door. "Come on in. It's awfully nice of you to do this for us. Can you join us for supper?"

"Oh, I don't want to intrude," said Molly as she set the basket and the thermos on the counter in the kitchen. Someone had set the kitchen table for three. It looked like they were hoping she would say yes. "But if you don't mind, I would love to stay."

Molly unpacked the picnic basket placing the items on the table and pouring the coffee into the waiting cups. Just as she got everything laid out, Steve came into the kitchen. He looked haggard but still had that wonderful smile that lit up his face. "I feel like pokey puppy," he said. "I smelled something wonderful as I woke up from a nap and wondered what my dad was fixing for supper that smelled so good."

"It's just meatloaf," said Molly. "Nothing very fancy I'm afraid."

"Meatloaf is my favorite. I even like to make meatloaf sandwiches with the leftovers."

They sat down to eat. As they passed the dishes around, Molly said to Chuck, "It must have been difficult raising a son all alone."

"We managed," said Chuck. "Steve was a great kid. He really pitched in and helped around the house when he got home from school. During the year we got along ok. But the first summer I realized after two weeks that a young boy cannot stay home by himself. My sister and her husband live in Decateur and she offered to have Steve come and stay with them for the summer. They had three boys and wanted Steve to come so that he could have someone to play with. I would go down on the weekends and stay with them. It all worked out. Donna's boys were older than Steve and they taught him a lot about sports. Really made him into the athlete he is today."

"Oh, I don't know, Dad," said Steve. "You spent an awful lot of time playing catch with me and teaching me how to bat and field the ball. If it hadn't been for you, I never would have made that first little league team."

They sat and reminisced as they finished their meal and started on the chocolate cake. When the meal was over, Molly put the leftovers in the refrigerator, threw away the disposable containers she had brought with her, and got ready to leave.

"I always like to do the dishes," she said with her tongue in her cheek.

"Thanks for the food and the conversation, Molly," said Steve. "It's so nice to have good friends in times like these."

"You're welcome," said Molly. "You'll be surprised how supportive this town can be. Everyone is feeling your pain, Steve. And we all wish we could make it go away. Call me if I can do anything for you."

Chapter 26

Three weeks later on Saturday, October 13, Ken, Sandy and their boys came over to Molly's to rake leaves. They brought rakes and appetites. Each started to work on their assigned area of the lawn raking the leaves into huge piles. About 11:30 when Sandy and Molly went into the kitchen to get lunch ready, Ken started the pile of leaves nearest the gazebo on fire. He went into the garage to get the long handled forks that his dad had made for roasting hot dogs when Ken was a little boy. He unrolled the garden hose and pulled it closer to the fire just in case.

Inside Sandy was chopping up the onions while Molly put the ketchup, mustard, and buns on the tray. Sandy took the huge bowl of potato salad out of the refrigerator where she had placed it when they arrived. Molly whipped up some hot chocolate. She had experimented with a lot of containers over the years and found that putting it in a couple of vacuum bottles kept it piping hot while they had their picnic out at the gazebo. She filled another tray with paper plates, tableware, thick white mugs, napkins, and bowls of graham crackers, marshmallows, and Hershey bars so they could make s'mores for dessert.

After lunch, the boys raked the piles of leaves into several large piles and started them on fire. Once that was done, they asked if they could go to the high school to catch the finish of the cross-country meet. Ken said he would keep an eye on the burning leaves if they wanted to run along.

"I'll think I'll go home and take a nap if you don't need me," said Sandy.

"Go ahead," replied Ken. "Take my truck. Mom can run me home when we're finished here."

"I'm worried about her," said Ken as Sandy drove out of the driveway. "She seems to be tired all the time lately."

"Well, she works full time at the flower shop and then has you and the boys to take care of when she's home. You all go at quite a clip. That's enough to wear anybody out," said Molly.

They sat in the gazebo and watched the flames devour the piles of leaves. Ken and she had always had lots of long conversations. The beautiful fall day, the smell of the burning leaves, and the gazebo brought back memories of all the years that they had been doing just this very thing.

As the fire died down and Ken got up to leave, he said, "The Crime Lab in Springfield sent us the results on the blood on the jacket we found at the Star Dust motel. It was the same blood type as Beth's. The jacket was purchased from Marshall Field's, but it is such a popular style that they don't keep records on who purchases them. It's an extra large and they found short, blond hair on the collar which goes along with Skip's description of the guy who checked in."

"Too bad his mother didn't make him sew a name tag in his clothes before he left for camp," Molly replied.

"This is no laughing matter," scolded Ken. "We also got information on the tire track we found at the golf course. Sid at the Goodyear store said that size tire would fit a pickup truck, a mini van, or an SUV. It was brand new which could mean the vehicle was new. We checked with Northend Garage to see if they had sold any new vehicles that fit that description lately. They said they hadn't, but to check the two dealerships in Milltown. I talked with Dick Thompson who owns the Chevy dealership there. He said they had sold two. The new chef at the golf course had traded in his Renault for a new Suburban and Pete Ryan bought a new Ventura for Connie. He also pointed out to me that the cast could've been made from one new tire on an old truck. I guess I'll check those two guys just in case to see where they were the day Beth was killed."

"Oh, what an awful thought," said Molly. "Why would either of them want to kill Beth?"

"I'm not sure they did, but I've got to eliminate every clue. By the way, did you know that Steve had taken out a million dollar life insurance policy on Beth?" Ken asked.

"Did she have a policy on Steve?" Molly replied.

"Yes," said Ken.

"Lots of business partners have policies like that so that if anything happens to one of them the business can go on. That hardly seems like a motive," said Molly.

Chapter 27

"One heart."

"One Spade."

"One No Trump."

"Pass."

"Two hearts."

"Pass" "Pass" "Pass"

They're your hearts, Peggy," said Angie as she led the Ace of Spades.

Molly laid down her dummy's hand and the play proceeded.

The Tuesday Bridge Club had asked Judy Phillips to take Beth's place. She had been a sub for several years, knew all the others, and seemed like the logical choice. She was playing with her partner, Nora, in Nora's dining room. The solid oak panel doors between the living room and the dining room in the 90-year-old Victorian house had been pushed open making them into one big room. Nora had decorated in shades of mauve and gray and pale blue which picked up the colors in the oriental rugs that lay atop the hard wood floors. The 12" baseboards, the banister of the staircase leading upstairs, the crown molding all gleamed in the sunshine of the lovely fall afternoon.

"Made five," said Angie. "Grossly underbid!"

"Oh, be quiet and deal," said Peggy as she gathered up the cards and handed them to Connie to shuffle.

"Three no trump," came from the living room.

"Five clubs."

"Pass." "Pass." "Pass."

"Five clubs to you," said Jenny. She lead the two of diamonds and hoped her partner Emily would be able to take a couple tricks since she had only six points in her hand.

"Down two," said Nora. "I should've let you have it for three no trump. I don't know what I was thinking. I just can't stop thinking about Beth's murder."

"Me either," said Jenny as they left the table and migrated into the kitchen to see if Molly had any news from Ken. They all stood around having a glass of lemonade while Molly filled them in.

"He and the boys were raking leaves at my house last Saturday, but he didn't have anything more than what's been in the <u>Bridgeville Harold</u> lately. They did find the murder weapon. It was a five iron that was stuck in Beth's golf bag. I guess Steve pointed out to Ken that Beth never left her clubs in the garage and he thought it was strange when he found them leaning against the wall out there. When they checked them out, they found a five iron that was too long to belong to five foot nothing Beth. They're checking it for fingerprints now."

Molly did not mention that they also checked Steve's golf bag to see if his five iron were missing.

Chapter 28

Molly walked into the kitchen, fastened her first prize – a gift certificate for a haircut at Jenny's beauty shop – to the refrigerator with a Bridgeville Realty magnate shaped like a house, and walked back toward the utility room near the garage to hang up her jacket. Just then the phone rang and she stopped to answer it.

"Hello, Molly, this is Chris. Chris Meinert. Dave and I are still planning to come up for the annual bridge tournament this weekend. The last time we talked, you suggested that we could stay with you. Does the offer still hold?"

"Chris! Hi! Of course. I've been cleaning like a madman getting ready for your visit. When are you coming?" cried Molly.

"We thought we'd arrive on Thursday about 4:00. We'd like to take you to the Four Aces for dinner."

"I'd love to go. Cheryl and Jim are staying here again this year too. But they're not coming until noon on Friday. I'm really looking forward to your visit. Every year they add another attraction for those no longer in the tournament. This year it's an antique car show. The cars have been arriving all week. It's such fun to see them driving around town."

"Can't wait! See you Thursday," said Chris. "Bye."

"Bye, bye," said Molly as she hung up the phone.

She hung up her jacket, picked up a laundry basket filled with sheets she had taken off the clothesline before going to Nora's, and went upstairs to make the beds.

She took the navy blue sheets into Ken's old room. Last year at the J. C. Penney's white sale she had indulged herself and bought new bedding. The navy sheets for this room were the same shade as the carpet and the navy, burgundy, and cream plaid bedspread and curtains looked great next to the freshly painted cream colored walls.

She gave the bed one last pat as she picked up the basket and headed to Kate's former room. She had purchased daffodil yellow sheets to match the carpet and walls in there. The comforter and the curtains were pale yellow covered with sprigs of green and yellow flowers. The pictures on the walls were watercolors of spring flowers that Kate had painted when she was in high school. The softness of the yellow just seemed to fit with the white wicker furniture.

"Might as well change my bedding while I'm at it," thought Molly as she walked down the hall to her room. The cream colored carpet from the family room and the living room continued up the stairs, down the hall and into Molly's room. The walls here were painted deep red and the bedspread and curtains were white with red rosebuds sprinkled here and there. The window seat looking out toward the river was covered with red material to match the walls and piled with cushions – some covered in solid red and some with the rosebud fabric. The red sheets were her final extravagance. Stepping back, she gave the room one last glance. "I love this room," she thought as she headed back to the laundry room to get fresh towels out of the dryer.

As she microwaved a bowl of stew that had been thawing all afternoon, she thought about the great cards she had been dealt at Nora's. "Sure hope I didn't use up all my good luck today," she thought as she sliced a loaf of French bread. "I'd like to see some pictures on the cards at the tournament this weekend."

Chapter 29

Friday. Tournament Day. Sun was shining and people were milling around the Big Ugly Building greeting old friends and checking the numbers on their ticket stubs against the brackets posted around the lobby to find out where they were to play their first game.

Molly had served her guests a Lasagna she had made last summer and stored in the freezer in the garage until today. Garlic bread, a tossed salad, and iced tea completed the meal. They ate at 4:00 in the afternoon and decided to forego dessert until later so they wouldn't be drowsy during the first round of the tournament.

At 6:00 they left Molly's and walked down River Road to the BUB. Cars were parked all up and down the road so there was no sense driving. Molly met Angie in the lobby and they walked down the hall to their first game. As they entered room 15, they looked around for the table with their names on it. They waved at Emily and Peggy who were standing by the table near the windows.

"Wouldn't it be funny if they were our opponents," said Angie as she studied the tables.

"I think they are," said Molly as they neared the windows and saw their name tags on the table there.

"Hello," smiled Emily. "Isn't this odd that we should be playing each other?"

"The luck of the draw," smiled Molly as she sat down opposite Angie and began to shuffle the cards.

Peggy spread the cards face down on the table and said "Let's draw for deal."

A two of diamonds, a four of clubs, a four of diamonds, and a Queen of Hearts for Emily. Molly handed her the deck of cards that she had shuffled and Peggy started shuffling the other deck. She put the made deck face down on her right, picked up her hand, and began sorting her cards as she heard her partner saying, "One diamond."

"One spade," said Molly.

"Two hearts," said Peggy.

"Two spades," said Angie.

"Three hearts," said Emily.

"Four spades," said Molly.

"Pass." "Pass." "Pass."

Peggy led the three of hearts, Angie laid down her hand as dummy, and Molly chose the jack of hearts from the dummy hand leaving a void in hearts there. Emily played the Ace of Hearts. Molly trumped the trick with the two of spades and she was off and running. She led the three of spades hoping to draw the two small trump that were out against her. She then proceeded to take all the rest of the tricks.

"Should've gone to slam with our bidding," said Angie as she shuffled the cards for the next hand.

At the end of the eighth hand, the scores were added up. Molly and Angie had won by a mere 150 points. Peggy and Emily got up to leave.

"Let's stop at The Four Aces and have a piece of hot fudge pecan pie," suggested Emily.

"Sounds good to me," said Peggy as they walked out of the room. She turned to wave at Angie and Molly and said, "Good luck! If it can't be us, hope you win it all!"

Molly and Angie walked out in the hall to check the brackets to see whom they played at the 9:30 session. The results weren't posted yet, so they walked down to the lobby for a glass of cider. As they drank the ice cold drink, they looked over the assortment of donuts and decided to pass since they were going back to Molly's for brownies and coffee later. They finished their cider and tossed the paper cups in the garbage can. When they checked the brackets again, they saw that their next game was in room 111 against a couple from Wisconsin. The first two hands were a disaster for Molly and Angie. By the third hand, things improved and they ended up winning by 50 points.

"Boy, we are just squeaking by, aren't we?" said Angie.

"Yep," said Molly, "but we're still in it, aren't we?"

"I guess we are," smiled Angie. "Let's go back to your house. I'm dying for one of your brownies."

They met Chris and Dave and Cheryl and Jim in the lobby and all walked home together by the light of the harvest moon. The crisp, fall weather felt good after being in the stuffy BUB all evening.

"We'll sleep good tonight," commented Dave as they neared Molly's driveway.

"How about some dessert and coffee first?" asked Molly.

"Sounds good," said Chris.

"Is it decaf?" asked Jim.

"It could be," said Molly as they reached the front door. She headed for the kitchen. The two men went in to the family room to watch the news on TV while the women went with Molly to set the table and pass out the brownies made from Aunt Cathy's recipe.

Finally the coffee was perked and they sat around the dining room table talking about the hands they'd played that evening. Everyone had survived the first two rounds and were going to play again at 8:00 a.m.

"Guess I'd better go home," yawned Angie. "We all need to get some sleep."

"I'll give you a ride home," said Molly. "Otherwise you'll meet yourself coming and going."

"O. K." responded Angie as they headed for the garage. Molly dodged around the cars in her driveway, dropped Angie off at her house in town, and went straight to bed when she got back home. It took her several minutes to unwind after the stimulating evening she'd had. Suddenly she realized that she hadn't brushed her teeth or washed her face so she got up, took care of those chores, and flopped into bed falling asleep almost immediately.

Aunt Cathy's Chocolate Brownies

4 oz unsweetened chocolate
2/3 cup shortening
2 cups sugar
4 eggs
1 teas. Vanilla
1 1/3 cup flour
1 tsp. Baking powder
1 tsp. Salt
1 cup nuts
9X13 pan

Heat oven to 350°   Grease 9 x 13 pan

Melt chocolate and shortening in a large sauce pan over low heat. Remove from heat. Mix in sugar, eggs, and vanilla. Stir in remaining ingredients. Spread in pan. Bake 30 minutes or until brownies begin to pull from side.

Chapter 30

The alarm went off at 6:30 and Molly woke up to the smell of coffee. "I didn't think I set my automatic coffee pot last night," she thought as she struggled into her red robe and scruffy slippers.

When she got to the kitchen, she found Chris sitting at the table drinking coffee and having a blueberry muffin. "M-m-m, these are great!" she exclaimed.

"I thought we'd be rushed this morning, so I bought a dozen at the Gingham Cat," said Molly as she poured coffee into a big white mug and selected a cranberry nut muffin. "Thanks for making the coffee," she said as she took a sip.

They finished their coffee as the rest of the group came downstairs. Putting their cups in the dishwasher, Molly and Chris went upstairs to dress. Soon everyone was ready and they headed back to the BUB for another round of bridge.

Angie was waiting for them in the lobby when they arrived. She and Molly were assigned to play in the cafeteria while Chris and Dave went to the gym and Jim and Cheryl went to the large conference room. They all agreed to meet at ll:30 to walk over to the Methodist Church for lunch.

Angie was the first dealer and won the bid with one spade. "One bids are always so hard to make," she said as her opponent led a heart.

Molly's dummy hand was of no help to Angie and they went down three. The next two hands went to the opponents. By the end of the eighth hand, it was obvious that Molly and Angie would not be playing in the next round.

It was a beautiful fall day, so they walked over to the band shell in the park and bought a glass of lemonade being sold there by the girls' track team. They sat in the Adirondack chairs down by the river and watched the water roll by. About 11:15, they strolled back to the BUB to meet the others. While they waited, they checked the schedule of events planned for that afternoon. The antique auto parade was to begin at 1:30 from the court house and proceed down Bridge Street to the park. St. Mary's Catholic Church was having bingo in the church hall at 2:30. The shuffle board tournament in the park was beginning at 3:00 and, of course, the walking tour was ongoing with maps available at Bridgeville Realty and the Chamber of Commerce.

They all decided during lunch that they would take the walking tour around town and look at the houses that were decorated especially for this weekend. After that, they would take naps at Molly's and return later to the park for the band concert since none of them had won that morning.

Supper at Molly's was Chicken Tetrazinni, salad, and piping hot biscuits whipped up with two cups of biscuit mix, one-quarter cup sugar and one-half can beer. It was such a beautiful afternoon that they decided to eat on the three-seasons porch.

The band concert was wonderful. They all marveled at how well the high school kids could play. A little Gershwin, a little Scott Joplin, some Bach and a lot of sing-a-long for audience participation.

When the concert ended, Cheryl suggested, "Let's walk down to the Sugar Plum for ice cream cones."

After several tastes using tiny pink spoons, they left the shop munching away on chocolate almond, butter pecan, fudge marble, orange sherbet and vanilla. They finished their cones in Molly's three-seasons room and turned in soon after.

The 10:30 church service at the Presbyterian Church was packed. Luckily they had arrived in time to get a seat. As the service progressed, they could smell pork chops cooking and decided to stay there for lunch. Long tables covered with white tablecloths and real china were set up in the Gathering Room. Platters of breaded pork chops were passed family style along with bowls of creamy scalloped potatoes, stewed tomatoes, lime Jell-O, and homemade bread. They decided to skip dessert since they had eaten way too much.

"He who indulges bulges," said Chris as they pushed themselves away from the table and headed for the BUB for the last round of the Tournament.

The final round started at 2:30. They took their seats in the bleachers and watched a couple from Kankakee beat a couple from Rockford. Everyone was pulling for the couple from Kankakee since he was 20 and she was his grandmother. At the end of the sixth hand, the score was even. The next hand, the young man and his grandmother won the bid with four hearts. The eighth hand was won by them also. The young man could've played it safe by ending the bidding at three no trump, but he upped it to four asking for aces. His grandmother responded five diamonds. He then bid five no trump. She responded six spades. His final bid was six no trump which they made with ease since his grandmother had 10 spades and a void in clubs. The applause was deafening as they were awarded the prize. The grandmother announced that her grandson was going to use the winnings to finish his college education at Southern Illinois University.

As Molly's guests put their suitcases in their cars, they expressed their gratitude for Molly's hospitality and made plans to return next year vowing to practice diligently so they would be the ones competing in the final round.

Molly waved a final goodbye as they pulled out of the driveway. Then she went inside to strip the beds and unload the dishwasher. Finishing her chores, she picked up the latest copy of the <u>Readers' Digest</u> and went out to the gazebo to relax and read and watch the leaves fall from the trees.

Claire's Chicken Tetrazinni

Serves 8
1. <u>Boil</u> chicken (hen is better) and bone to bite sizes
2. <u>Saute</u> until soft:
> 1 Chopped Green Pepper
> 2 sticks chopped celery
> 1 stick butter

3. <u>Stir</u> in to make a paste:
> 4 TBS. sifted flour

4. <u>Add</u>:

> 2 cups room temperature milk
> 2 cans cream of mushroom soup (undiluted)
> 2 4 oz cans sliced mushrooms
> pimiento (optional)
> 1 minced garlic clove
> 1 tsp. Worchester sauce
> ½ cup wine (cooking sherry)

5 <u>Mix</u> until smooth

6. <u>Add</u> 1 cup at a time stirring until smooth:

> 3½ cups American or cheddar or Velvetta cheese

7. <u>Fold</u> in:
> ¾ lb. Cooked spaghetti

8. <u>Stir</u> in boned chicken.

9. <u>Heat</u> through and top with shredded cheese, slivered almonds and sliced mushrooms if desired.

Chapter 31

Jimmy was so excited about going to ITT. He took his schedule out of his wallet the minute he got home and pinned it to the bulletin board hanging on the wall near his desk. He must've looked at that schedule a hundred times or more in the last month and every time he looked at it he thought about Gina.

He finally got up the nerve to ask Grady O'Mera if he could have three days off, took the $50 Molly had left for him out of the cash register, and headed back to Chicago. He pulled into the parking garage at 11:35 and drove around and around until he finally found a parking place on the third floor. By the time he ran down three flights of stairs and waited for the walk sign to cross the street, it was five minutes to 12. As he ran into the Administration Building, he had a frantic thought. "What if she's not here today?" He rounded the corner just in time to see her putting on her coat.

"Hey!" he said as he neared her window.

"Hey!" she responded. "You're, uh, Jimmy, isn't it?"

"Yea. That's me. I thought maybe we could go to lunch or something."

"Oh, I'm sorry," she said. "I've got a dentist appointment today. But I don't have any plans for dinner. How about that?"

"Great," he said beaming from ear to ear. "Should I pick you up here or at your apartment, or where?"

"Pick me up at my apartment. I'll be ready about six o'clock. Is that ok with you?"

"Perfect," he said as they walked out of the building and down the sidewalk. Gina's car was parked in the faculty lot. As she drove away, he headed for her apartment building. He decided to leave his car where it was and walk the few blocks. It was a nice day for a walk and besides he had nothing to do until six o'clock except check on the status of his living arrangements.

Striding into the office, he spied the rental agent talking to a perspective renter.

"I'll be right with you," she said to Jimmy.

"No rush," he replied as he looked at the notices pinned to the bulletin board. It looked like half the people living here needed rides someplace for Thanksgiving. Thank goodness he had his own car. Maybe one of these guys would like to buy his pickup. It was a little rusty, but it did have a new set of tires and he wouldn't be needing two vehicles once he started school.

"OK, young man. What can I do for you?" asked the rental agent as she walked across the moss green carpet toward him.

"I just came to check on that vacancy that's coming up," replied Jimmy.

"What was your name again?" she asked.

"Jimmy. Jimmy Reed," he said.

She turned to her desk and thumbed through a card file of applications sitting on the right hand corner next to the phone.

"Let's see," she said. "Ah, yes. Well, George still hasn't moved out. His lease is up the first of November, but he's asked if he could stay two more weeks. How does that fit with your plans?"

"That's good for me. That'll give me plenty of time to get settled in before classes start on December 4. Do you want me to give you some money today?" he asked.

120

"Why don't you give me a check and I'll hold it until you're ready to move in?" she said.

"I don't have a checking account yet," Jimmy replied turning a deep shade of red. "What a hick she must thing I am," he thought, "coming up here without a checking account."

"Well, why don't you open one?" she asked. "There's a branch office of Bank One about two blocks from here. Lots of our renters bank there. It's handy and I think pretty reasonable too.

"OK. Thanks," said Jimmy. "Which way do I go?"

She pointed him in the right direction and he started out. Before he got to the end of the sidewalk, he turned around and came back. Sticking his head in the door he said, "Thanks. Thanks a lot," waved his hand, and headed back to his quest for the bank.

Just as he was leaving the building, Allen was coming home for lunch.

"Hey, Jimmy," he said extending his hand to give his old basketball rival a handshake. "Are you here for a visit?"

"Just for a couple days," replied Jimmy.

"Well, hey, why don't you stay with us. George is gone for a couple days looking for an apartment closer to his new job. This'll give you a chance to see if you'll fit in with us."

"Hey, that'd be great," said Jimmy. "I'd love that. I'm taking Gina out for dinner, but I need a place to crash after that."

"Well, what are you doing now?" asked Allen.

"I'm on my way to open a checking account," replied Jimmy.

"There's a Burger King right next door to the bank and we both have to eat. Come on. I'll walk down that way, we'll grab some lunch, and then you can go to the bank and I'll head back to my classes."

"Sounds good to me. I could go for a whopper and some fries," said Jimmy as they turned and walked down the walk.

That night at dinner he was telling Gina about his adventure of opening an account.

"It was really pretty painless," he said as he rolled the spaghetti around on his fork. The table was covered with a red and white checked cloth, a Chianti bottle covered with wax that had dripped from the candle stuck in its neck sat in the middle of the table, and two plates heaped with spaghetti and meat balls sat in front of them. The rich aroma of garlic filled the air as Gina pulled open the napkin in the basket to take out another piece of bread.

"Why, were you worried about it?" she asked as she sunk her teeth into the buttery slice.

"Well, I've never had a checking account before. This is all new to me," he said as he popped a vinegar and oil covered cherry tomato from his tossed salad into his mouth.

"You're in for a lot of firsts from now on," she said.

They chatted through dinner prolonging it as long as they could with coffee and zoupa englaise that melted in their mouths.

Gina invited him to come in and watch TV for a while. About 12:00, he said goodnight and walked across the hall. Thank goodness he had made arrangements with Allen to sleep on his couch.

The next morning, he and Gina went out for breakfast before she went to work and he headed back to Bridgeville. What a great time he had had. One more month and he would be living there. He couldn't wait.

As he was driving along dreaming of what his life would be like, it began to rain. Just south of Kankakee it started to pour. He reached down to turn on his windshield wipers and lights and noticed that his gas gauge was on a quarter full. Surely he'd have enough to get home. He'd spent most of his $50 eating out and just didn't have much left for gas. Things were going just fine until he passed the golf course on the outskirts of Bridgeville. Just a little farther and he'd be at the Shell station. He hated driving past that golf course. Every time he did it reminded him of the day they found Beth's body. Just a little farther now and he'd be safe and sound at home.

"Oh, please. Help me not to run out of gas here."

Chapter 32

Rick James strolled into Reverend Brown's study and plopped his lanky frame into the chair next to Rev. Brown's desk.

"I got the leaky faucet in the ladies bathroom fixed, the thermocouple on the pilot light on the hot water heater replaced, and the kitchen floor mopped. It's raining too hard to wash the windows in the parsonage or to rake leaves. It's almost lunchtime and I'd like to take you out. Kinda a thank you for letting me use your car while my truck was in the shop."

"Why, Rick. What a nice surprise. I'd love to go to lunch with you. But it's not necessary for you to treat."

"No really. I want to. When I asked to borrow your wheels, I didn't know it would take so long to fix mine. I thought maybe we could go out to the country club. I hear they got some new cook out there that is really good."

"Sounds good to me. Let me wash my hands and I'll be ready to go," said Rev. Brown as he pushed his chair back and headed for the bathroom.

"I'll get my truck and meet you around in the front," shouted Rick to the pastor as he walked down the hall.

Chapter 33

The phone rang as Molly was having her second cup of coffee and paying a few bills.

"Molly?" said Nora. "It's me. Nora. I'm just finishing my shift in the hospital gift shop and thought since it's too nasty to work on your flowers maybe we could go to the golf course for lunch. I could go for a nice quiche."

"Wonderful idea," said Molly. "Give me half an hour to get my face on."

Molly left her bills and her checkbook on the table as she ran upstairs to change her clothes. She put on her Navy slacks and her yellow and blue print blouse. She grabbed her yellow slicker from a peg in the laundry room as she headed for the garage. She pushed the button to activate the garage door opener, climbed into her car, and backed out into the rain.

"Thank goodness for modern conveniences," thought Molly. "I'd be drenched if I had to get out and close that door in this downpour."

She drove down River Road, turned into the golf course parking lot, pulled up the hood on her slicker and made a dash for the door trying not to step into any puddles on the way. Nora was already sitting at a table by the fireplace. Molly stopped to say hello to Rev. Brown and Rick James who were sitting at the table next to Nora's. Hanging her slicker on the back of her chair, she sat down and said to Nora, "What a good idea! Thanks for calling me."

Nora said, "Can't think of anyone I'd rather be with on a dreary day. You've always been there to brighten my life, Molly."

"Hello, ladies," said Betty as she poured water into their glasses. "What'll you have today?"

"Do you have quiche today?" asked Nora.

"Yes, we do," replied Betty. "And we have fresh crab cakes or crepes stuffed with chicken a la king."

"Oh, the crab cakes sound good to me," said Molly. "And a cup of hot tea."

"I'll have the quiche," said Nora. "And the tea sounds good to me also."

As Betty left, Nora and Molly chatted about what was selling at the gift shop these days, how hard it was to get volunteers to work there, and finally about the last bridge game at Nora's. They both agreed that Judy was a nice addition to the club. When their food arrived, they stopped talking long enough to savor the delicious blend of flavors. As they ate, they noticed that Jean-Claude was working his way around the dining room stopping to chat with the diners here and there. When he stopped to talk to Rick and Rev. Brown, Nora leaned over and whispered to Molly,

"Remember a couple weeks ago when we were having coffee at my house and you asked me if I saw anything at Beth's house the day of her murder? Well, I thought about it after you left and I think I did see a truck leave that morning, but Steve has a dark truck and I guess I didn't pay any attention. After talking to you, I remembered that Steve was in New York and Beth didn't like to drive his truck. Maybe I could talk to Ken about this. Would you go with me tomorrow?"

"Sure," said Molly. "I'll call him when I get home and I'll let you know what time would be good for him."

Just then a shadow fell across the white tablecloth. They glanced up to see a tall, broad shouldered man with twinkling blue eyes and perfect teeth smiling down at them.

"Allo, ladies," he said with just a hint of a French accent. "I'm the new chef here, Jean-Claude Ganyo. How was your lunch?"

"It was delicious," beamed Nora. "I'm Nora Beck and this is my friend Molly Donner."

"Allo, Mollee" Jean-Claude said as he raised her hand to his lips.

"We've heard so much about you," said Molly as she reluctantly withdrew her hand from his. It wasn't every day she got attention from a good-looking young man and she was rather enjoying it.

"It's nice to finally meet you. I must say you've done wonders with this dining room. It looks beautiful and the food has never been this good."

"Thank you so much. You're too kind," said Jean-Claude as he moved away from their table moving toward the table where Steve Sheridan and several other local businessmen were just finishing their lunch.

Chapter 34

Rick and Rev. Brown finished their BLTs, coleslaw, and apple pie, paid the bill and headed for town. About half way there they spotted a car pulled off on the shoulder and a young man standing in the pouring rain.

"Pull over," said Rev. Brown. "Let's see if we can help."

Rick pulled in behind the parked car and rolled his window down a crack. The young man approached the car and leaned down to peer in the window.

"Hi, Rick. Hi, Rev. Brown," he said. "Could you give me a lift into town?"

"Hi, Jimmy," said Rev. Brown. "What's the problem?"

"I'm outta gas," replied Jimmy.

"You work at a gas station and you ran out of gas?" said Rick.

"Yea. I'm on my way home from Chicago. I got so many things on my mind about school that I didn't check my gas gauge. Pretty dumb, huh?" He climbed in the back seat of Rick's truck and they pulled out onto River Road just as Molly and Nora drove past.

"Do you think you could drop me off at the church first?" asked Rev. Brown. "I've got a young couple coming in to talk about their wedding and I want to be there when they arrive at 2:00."

"O.K. by me," said Rick. They dropped Rev. Brown off, drove around the block, and headed for the Shell station. As they drove down Washington Street, they saw Ken Donner walking up the sidewalk to Nora's front door.

"I wonder what the sheriff's doing at Mrs. Beck's," said Jimmy.

"Rev. Brown and me heard her say to Sheriff Donner's mother at lunch that she'd seen something at Sheridan's the day Mrs. Sheridan was found dead in her dining room," said Rick.

"Saw something?" asked Jimmy. "Did she say what?"

"Nope," responded Rick. Just said she wanted to talk to the sheriff soon."

Chapter 35

Nora and Molly ran through the rain to their cars and headed home. Molly turned in her driveway and waved at Nora as she went by. The phone was ringing as Molly walked into her kitchen.

"Hello," said Molly.

"Hi, Molly. This is Connie. I'm just calling to see if you could work for an hour or two in the concession stand at the ballgame on Saturday."

"Sure," said Molly. "What time?"

"The game starts at 11:00 and the concession stand opens at 10:00. How about helping set up from 9:00 to 10:00?"

"That would be fine. I'll see you on Saturday. Bye"

"Bye," said Connie.

Molly hung up then picked up the receiver and dialed Ken's office. "Hello, Bernice," she said. "This is Molly Donner. Is Ken there?"

"He just got back from lunch," said Bernice. "I'll put you through to his office."

"Hello, Mom," said Ken. "What can I do for you?"

Every time she heard his voice Molly thought how much like his father he was: broad shoulders, light brown hair cut short, soft brown eyes so dark that you could barely see the pupils, strong, sturdy hands and that wonderful voice.

"Oh, Ken," she said. "I'm so glad I caught you. I had lunch with Nora today and she would like to talk with you. She thinks she may have seen someone leaving Beth's."

"I have some time this afternoon unless there's an emergency. How bout if I drop by her house around 2:00?"

"That sounds perfect," said Molly. "Would you mind if I joined you?"

"I don't care if Nora doesn't mind," replied Ken. "I'll see you at 2:00." And with that he hung up.

Molly called Nora to tell her to expect them at 2:00 and then spent the next half-hour finishing the bill paying she had left spread on the table.

At 2:00 sharp Molly pulled up behind Ken's police car parked in front of Nora's house. Nora opened the door and she and Molly walked into the study where Ken was already seated in front of the fireplace drinking a cup of coffee.

"Hi, Mom," he said.

"Hello, Ken," responded Molly as she sat down and accepted the coffee cup Nora was handing her. Helping herself to a chocolate chip cookie from the plate on the coffee table she listened as Ken told them about the medical examiner's report which showed that Beth had definitely been killed elsewhere and her body moved to her house. That's why there was so little blood at the house. The killer must've dropped her off sometime before 9:30 since she had been at Jenny's getting her hair frosted at 6:00 a.m. and had rented a golf cart at the golf course at 7:45.

"Around 9:30?" asked Nora. "I was cleaning up the breakfast dishes around that time. My kitchen window looks across the alley and right into Sheridan's back yard. Oh my gosh! I could've seen the killer!"

"Well, don't broadcast that," said Molly. "They still don't know who did this. He might be listening if you tell someone."

"Do you think it's somebody who lives in Bridgeville?" asked Nora.

"I don't know," said Ken, "but it could be."

"Well, I did see a dark pickup type vehicle pull out of their driveway about 9:45, but I didn't see who was driving."

"Did you notice the license plate number?" asked Ken.

"No, I thought that Steve had returned from New York a couple days earlier than planned so I didn't look at the truck too closely," said Nora.

Chapter 36

Along the grassy banks of the Iroquois River and in the shadow of the Milltown Bridge lay Charles O. Granfield park. Mr. Granfield was a local farmer who had struck natural gas on his farm while drilling a new water well in the late 1930's. He believed so strongly that physical activity kept young people out of trouble, that he donated a large portion of his newfound wealth to building a community park complete with two ball diamonds, six tennis courts, a picnic shelter, a playground, and a swimming pool.

On Saturday, October 27, the high school baseball team held its annual fundraiser. Every year the old timers would get together and play the Bridgeville High School varsity baseball team at Granfield Park. The various restaurants furnished the food for the concession stand and since Connie Ryan was in charge, most of the Tuesday Bridge Club volunteered to work. All the proceeds from the sale of the tickets and the food went toward funding the baseball team's equipment and uniforms for the next year. Not only was it profitable but it was also fun. Everyone in town looked forward to the game.

Molly got to the field about 9:00 to help set up. Rick James and Steve Sheridan were there setting up the concession stand which consisted of saw horses set up in a large square with sheets of plywood screwed on to them. The Four Aces restaurant sold sandwiches and lemonade on one side; the Gingham Cat sold muffins, tea, and coffee on another side; Matty's Malt Shop sold hamburgers, hot dogs, popcorn, soft drinks and milk shakes on a third side; and this year Jean-Claude from the golf course had the fourth side where he would be selling French pastries and crepes. Everything was set up by 10:00 and people started arriving about 10:30. The mayor threw out the first pitch at 11:00 sharp. Jimmy Reed got the popcorn machine cranked up and soon the smell of freshly popped popcorn wafted over the field. People began drifting out to the stand to get something to eat. Molly and Nora were busy pouring coffee and warming muffins in the toaster oven when Jenny Wilcox and Peggy Fitch showed up to relieve them.

"How's the game going?" inquired Molly as she wiped her hands on a paper towel.

"7 to 1," replied Peggy. "The high school team has 7."

"Come on, Nora," said Molly. "We can come back and get something to eat later. We need to go out there and cheer on the old timers!"

"O. K.," said Nora. "But let's not wait too long. Smelling all these yummy smells is making me hungry."

Chapter 37

As he worked around the concession stand he thought to himself, *"I've got to get rid of that gabby Nora Beck before she tells the whole world what she saw the morning of Beth's death. This would be a perfect place with all these people around. They wouldn't be able to tell who did it and maybe they'd just think it was something she ate."* He looked around to see if there was anything there he could use when he spied the little shed where the ball diamond equipment was kept.

"Maybe there's something in there," he thought.

He walked slowly over to the shed, opened the door and slipped inside. As he looked around the shelves, he spied a box of rat poison shoved back in the corner. Picking it up carefully, he poured a large portion of it into his handkerchief and put it into his pocket. He got back to the concession stand just as Molly and Nora were buying their lunch.

"Now's my chance," he thought.

Chapter 38

Connie was watching the changing of the volunteers thinking about what a nice town Bridgeville was to live in. So many nice people willing to help out. All you had to do was ask. She loved being part of the annual ballgame.

Connie and Pete had been very successful here and very happy. The highlight of Connie's year was the day she was asked to join the Tuesday Bridge Club. What a great group of women. And here they all were again for the umpteenth year volunteering to help the baseball team raise money. As she stood looking out at the baseball diamond, she saw someone come out of the tool shed wiping his hands on his handkerchief.

"I wonder what he was doing in there?" she thought to herself.

Molly and Nora went to sit next to Steve Sheridan and his dad in the bleachers and root for the old timers who were losing 7-1. About the 7th inning, they decided to get something to eat. Molly headed for The Four Aces to get a ham sandwich from Connie Ryan. Nora got a hot dog from Matty and said to Molly, "Want to split a chocolate éclair?"

"No," said Molly. "I want a whole one. Let's each get one."

They loaded up their sandwiches with condiments and returned to their seats. Soon the bases were loaded and Andy Durant, who had graduated from high school last year and was the newest member of the old timers team, was up to bat. He hit a grand slam and everyone stood up to cheer as they rounded the bases. Everyone except Nora that is. She had slumped over in her seat. When the cheering stopped Molly and Angie sat down and realized that Nora was ill. Molly ran down to the home side dugout where the EMS people were sitting. They reacted quickly – one running back to the stands with Molly and the other going to get the stretcher out of the ambulance. As they loaded Nora into the ambulance, she was barely breathing. Molly climbed in to ride along and hold her hand if she needed it. When they got to the hospital, Molly went to admitting to fill out the forms and to call Nora's husband, Art. She went upstairs and sat next to the bed looking at her friend hooked up to tubes and monitors. Just then Nora's eyes fluttered and she raised her head. Molly leaned over and Nora tried to whisper but just let out a big sigh. With that she closed her eyes and sank back on the pillow. By the time Art got there, her breathing was labored and her lips were turning blue. Within a half hour, she was dead.

Chapter 39

Working next to Connie in those close confines was torture. Seeing that frosted hair, hearing that tinkling laugh, smelling that fresh, clean perfume she always wore. It was torture. He had put the rat poison in the food he served Nora. Now he had to get rid of Connie – his real target in the first place. He realized that she was never going to leave her husband. He was going to be doomed to watch her grow old with another man. He just couldn't take it.

He lay in his bed unable to sleep, thoughts bouncing around in his mind. Slowly pieces of the puzzle started falling into place. Soon he fell asleep, secure in the feeling that Connie would not be sleeping with Pete Ryan this time next week. In fact, she'd never sleep with anyone ever again. If he couldn't have her, no one could have her.

Chapter 40

As Nora and Molly pulled away from the park in the ambulance, the umpire called the game. Everyone headed for the parking lot in silence. Connie, Pete, Jean-Claude, Matty, Rick James, Jimmy Reed, and Carol Ann Kempton packed the food away and took the concession stand down, stowing the sawhorses and plywood in the tool shed for next year. All this was done in stony silence as they moved around dazed by the events of the day.

Connie and Pete took the left over food back to The Four Aces and put it in the cooler. They checked with Dotty, the manager in charge, to see if everything was running smoothly there and headed for the hospital. They arrived there just in time to see Art and Molly driving out of the parking lot.

"That does not look good," said Pete. "If she was alive, they would've stayed."

"Oh, Pete. She can't be dead. Not Nora! Who would want to kill her? She's the sweetest person in Bridgeville."

They parked the car and walked into the Emergency Room. Ken Donner was talking to Dr. Westerman as they entered. Pete asked the nurse at the registration desk what Nora's status was.

"I'm so sorry to tell you this," she replied. "She didn't make it."

Pete walked back to Connie, put his arms around her and held her tight as she sobbed as though her heart would break. They rode home quietly, walked into the living room, poured themselves a drink and sat on the couch arms around each other talking and talking trying to figure out what was going on in Bridgeville.

Later as Connie slid into the tub trying to soak away the problems of the day, she kept thinking about what she had seen at the concession stand. What was he doing in the tool shed? Did that have anything to do with Nora's death? The more she was around him, the more she had the feeling that she knew him from somewhere else grew. It was really creepy and very frustrating not being able to place him.

Chapter 41

Art and Molly rode back to the ball diamond in silence. As Molly got out of his car, she said, "I'm so sorry, Art. I can't believe she's gone. She's been a part of my life for as long as I can remember. I'll be at home. Call me if you need someone to talk to."

Molly got into her car and drove slowly home trying not to cry. As the garage door closed slowly, she vowed to herself that she was going to find this killer if it was the last thing she did. Two friends of hers were dead and that was two too many.

Ken came by later in the evening and said that the Medical Examiner had called him. The autopsy showed that Nora was poisoned. He said, "Looks like arsenic. The only food in her stomach was a hot dog and chocolate éclair so whatever killed her she ate it at the ball diamond."

"Killed at the ball diamond by the bridge," said Molly. "Beth was killed by the bridge over the creek at the golf course. Do you think there's a pattern here?"

"Well, one was killed with a club, and the next one at the diamond and both were members of your Tuesday Bridge Club. Do you know anyone that has an ax to grind with you ladies?" asked Ken.

"No, replied Molly. "Those were two of the best-liked women in town. I can't imagine that anyone would want to kill them."

"For a while I thought that Beth was killed because of jealousy," said Ken. "She'd been working out with Jimmy Reed. I considered an affair gone sour or her husband getting jealous of the time they spent together. Nora's death sorta puts a new spin on that theory though. Unless the two deaths are unrelated."

"Oh, Ken," cried Molly. "There couldn't have been anything going on between Beth and Jimmy. That sounds so sordid."

"Well, there's nothing nice about murder and we've had two of them here in the past month," said Ken.

Chapter 42

The day dawned gray and overcast. The doors to the church opened and closed as the people entered for Nora's funeral. Almost everyone in town was there since Nora had touched their lives in one way or another. From the recipients of aid from the Red Cross disaster team Nora chaired to the Board of Directors of the Bank, Nora was known and loved by all. Well not quite all. Someone had disliked her enough to poison her.

Art, his daughter, Barbie, and her family, and his son Bob with his wife and two children sat in the front row. The Tuesday Bridge Club and their families sat in the second and third rows. The rest of the church was full to overflowing. Some people had to stand in the back by the coat racks, some in the foyer, and some even had to stand on the front steps. The choir sang some of Nora's favorite hymns: Just a Closer Walk With Thee, Sweet Hour of Prayer, and In The Garden. How many times had Molly sat next to Nora in church as they were growing up singing those songs? They sat next to each other in church, in school, and at basketball games.

Starting in the sixth grade, they had gone to every single game. Molly's brother, Patrick, and Seth had been seniors that year and Bridgeville had a wonderful team. Nora and Molly liked to get to the games early so they could sit in the front row. They watched the JV team warm up, but by the time the game started, adults had moved into the front rows and the two girls had to move up higher. When the varsity game started, they had their backs against the press box at the top of the bleachers and the rest of the gym was filled with cheering fans – the high school cheering section to their left and the opposing team's fans to their right. They dreamed of the day when they would be able to sit in the Bridgeville cheering section.

Molly's dad drove to all the away games to watch Patrick play and he took Nora and Molly with him. Both Patrick and Seth went to Northern Illinois University after graduation and Molly's dad would often take the girls up to DeKalb to watch the games. By the time Molly was a Freshman at Northern, Patrick and Seth had graduated and were teaching school – Patrick in St. Charles and Seth in Elgin. They came back to campus occasionally to watch their old teammates play. After the game they would take Molly to the PUB for hamburgers and cokes. By Molly's Senior year, Seth was making the trip to DeKalb even when there wasn't a basketball game. After Molly graduated, they married and moved into Seth's apartment in Elgin where Molly got a job teaching English in the Middle School.

At the end of the year, Seth's dad called to tell them about the openings for teachers at Bridgeville High. Without a moment's thought, they both applied for jobs there, accepted them when they were offered, and moved back to their home town to renew old friendships. Naturally, Nora and her husband were the first people Molly and Seth had over for dinner in their newly rented house. What a wonderful, life-long friend Nora had been. How empty Molly's life was going to be without her.

Rev. Brown gave the eulogy and several people had asked him if they could speak. The couple she let stay rent free in a little house she owned until they had enough money saved to make a down payment; the director of Meals on Wheels who said if it hadn't been for Nora's vision and encouragement, the project would never have gotten off the ground; the Art Director who reminded them of Nora's love of theater, her involvement in the creation of the community theater group, and the staging of their first production on a make-shift platform in her backyard to a very limited audience that had to bring their own lawn chairs. As the stories unfolded, those in attendance thought privately of the ways Nora's life had touched their own and how deeply they would all miss her.

The funeral procession wound its way down Bridge Street from the church to the cemetery. Molly noticed that not a business in town was open. Even the Northend Garage was closed. As they drove past she saw Jake and Rick James standing by the office in suits and white shirts watching the cars file by.

Merri Borkowski

Chapter 43

Homecoming was always a busy day for the Bridgeville Police Department. Ken Donner was driving around on patrol as were Dean, Scott, and a couple state police cars. Too often alums would get together for a beer or two and wind up too drunk to drive home safely.

Rick wedged his way into Micky's Arcade. "Everybody must've come here after the game," he thought as he put his money up on the bar. "Why does everybody think Homecoming is so special?"

"Gimme a beer here will ya, Micky?" he shouted over the music from the jukebox. He took a big swallow from his glass and looked down the bar at the blond sitting about four stools from him. Was that her? Was that Connie Ryan? He wished he could see better. He squinted through the smoke. Boy, she was a fox! And nice too. Working with her in the concession stand had been great. He'd like to be with her more. Maybe he could get a job at The Four Seasons. Then he could see her all the time. Just then a tall guy walked up to the blond, whispered something to her, and they walked out together. As they passed Rick, he could see that it wasn't Connie.

"I've got to get outta here," he thought. "I'm beginning to see her everywhere. I've had enough to drink anyway."

He walked out to the parking lot, got into his truck and started to pull out into traffic. As he sat waiting for his chance, he looked in his rearview mirror.

"Damn! I'm busted." he said outloud as he saw Ken Donner sitting right behind him, lights flashing.

Rick parked his truck and headed for the police cruiser. As Ken was putting him into the back seat of his cruiser, a large wad of bills fell out of Rick's pocket and landed at Ken's feet. After locking Rick up for the night, Ken counted the money - $2200. What a coincidence.

Chapter 44

The Sunday before Thanksgiving, Molly sat in church listening to Rev. Brown's sermon about being thankful. "Even though we are going through some trying times here in Bridgeville, we still have much to be thankful for: this beautiful, sunny day; the fellowship of good friends; good health; and on Thursday we'll all be thankful for good appetites when we sit down to the magnificent meals prepared by those we love."

"He's right," thought Molly. "Especially about good friends." Out of the corner of her eye she could see Art and his daughter Barbie and wondered how they were getting along. After the service, she stopped to talk to Peggy Fitch for a minute. Art joined them and as Peggy moved on down the sidewalk, Art said to Molly,

"Isn't this a gorgeous day? I heard they have a great brunch at The Four Aces. Would you like to join Barbie and me? I haven't done much since Nora died except go to work. This was the kind of day she loved so much that I hate to waste it."

"I'd love to," replied Molly. "Why don't we both drive since it's on my way home? Then we won't have to come clear back here to get my car after lunch."

"OK," said Art. "We'll meet you there."

They parked their cars in the parking lot alongside the restaurant and walked up the flagstone walk to the front door of the restaurant. As they walked, Molly asked Barbie what she was doing these days.

"I live in Moline." Barbie said. "My husband is an accountant for John Deere. Our two girls are in high school, so we're busy with lots of school activities. And of course, being a child of my mother, I play bridge once a month with a wonderful group of ladies."

The huge double entry doors were thrown open inviting guests to enter. The flagstone continued as the floor of the foyer linking inside to outside. The walls and the seven-foot ceiling were paneled with reddish-brown mahogany that shone from years of handrubbing with beeswax polish. The brass sconces on the walls softly illuminated the burnished mahogany ceiling giving the effect of entering a cozy room. To the right was the former family parlor now filled with diners laughing, chatting and enjoying the brunch. Behind the parlor overlooking the river was the screened-in porch which was open to diners on days like today when the air was warm and the sunlight sparkled on the water.

Straight ahead was the stairway to the second and third floors where the restaurant manager, Dotty Billings, and her husband Malcolm, better known by everyone in town as Bill, lived with their three children. Dotty may manage the restaurant, but Bill did everything else. He mowed acres of grass, planted flowers in the beds around the house so that every season looked better than the last, and raised all the vegetables and most of the fruit used in the restaurant. Besides these duties, he could repair almost everything that went wrong in the old Bartholomew House.

As Art, Barbie and Molly turned to the left, they walked through the huge archway into what once was the living room. The ten-foot ceiling was a mass of structural wooden beams criss-crossing the room. The far wall was a fireplace made of large fieldstones with a wood beam for a mantle. The original carpet had been removed and the hardwood floor reflected the flickering fire in the fireplace. A long buffet table had been moved from one wall and placed in the center of the room. People were slowly moving around it filling their plates with steaming piles of scrambled eggs, crisp slices of bacon, sausage, French toast swimming in real maple syrup, biscuits and sausage gravy, hash-browned potatoes fried with little bits of onion for taste, and fried apples cooked with cinnamon and sugar. At one end of the table were platters filled with slices of cantaloupe, watermelon, and strawberries, bowls of raspberries and grapes, and today there was fresh pineapple flown in from Hawaii.

Dotty greeted them at the door and lead them to a table in the original dining room overlooking the river. "Just help yourself," she said. "I'll bring the water and drinks. Coffee for everyone?"

They all nodded in agreement and stepped up to the buffet table plates in hand. As they ate, they sat looking at the river and chatting about what a beautiful Indian Summer day it was. Soon Connie stopped by with the coffee pot for refills and said to Molly,

"Don't forget that bridge is at my house on Tuesday. I'm anxious for everyone to see what we've done with our remodeling. Come early if you can and I'll show you around."

"Oh, I'll be there," replied Molly with a smile.

Chapter 45

Connie finished dusting the sideboard in the dining room and glanced around to see if everything was in order. It was her turn to entertain the Tuesday Bridge Club and she wanted to be sure everything was perfect. She had made the tomato bisque in September using the last of the fresh tomatoes from the huge garden at the Four Aces and froze it until today. It was bubbling away in the crockpot on the island in her country kitchen. Baskets, dried flowers and herbs hung from the dark beams overhead. The shiny copper pots hung on the rack over the cooktop on the island. The large terra cotta squares of tile on the floor and the dark pine cupboards with the white porcelain knobs combined to make the kitchen a cozy as well as functional place. She had tried out many new recipes here before including them on the menu at The Four Aces.

Connie pulled back the white café curtain in the leaded window over the sink and peered around the geraniums in the window box to see if a car had pulled into the driveway. No one there. Funny. She had the feeling that someone had pulled up.

She walked back into the dining room to put two decks of cards, tallies, and a score pad on the table. She thought she'd have four play there and four play at the kitchen table in the breakfast nook rather than set up a card table in the living room where they had just installed toast-colored carpet. She didn't want to risk any accidental spills. The carpet looked so gorgeous with the antique pine furniture and the dark woodwork.

She loved living in this house. It had once been the gardener's cottage when Phinnias Bartholomew lived in his house. Built of Indiana limestone, the cottage blended into the hillside of the riverbank in the shadow of the Milltown bridge. Pete and she had lived on the second floor of The Four Aces when they first moved to town. As soon as they finished renovating the restaurant, they started on the cottage. As they cleared the weeds and brambles from the yard, they found yellow and red rose bushes, huge, bushy peonies, and lots of moss roses growing near the flagstone patio facing the river. The next spring they were delighted to see tulips and crocus coming up near the house and the field between the cottage and the restaurant was a sea of daffodils.

She walked up the newly carpeted stairs to the second floor. They had just added a master bedroom, master bath, and a guest bedroom with its own bath. The original cottage was a one-floor dwelling. The bedroom which had been on that floor, Connie and Pete made into a dining room. The remodeling had almost doubled the amount of space in the house.

She checked her make-up and gave her hair a quick brush. As she looked at herself in the mirror, she thought "Am I too old for this hairdo? I haven't changed since I was in high school. Maybe it's time for something new. I wonder what I'd look like if my hair wasn't frosted. Maybe I'll ask Jenny for some suggestions."

Just then a face appeared in the mirror next to hers and a hand covered her mouth to keep her from screaming. A gun was pointed at her head. The voice said, "Don't scream and I'll take my hand away."

"What do you want?" she gasped.

"You," he said. "I've always wanted you. Ever since we were Freshmen in college, I've dreamed of having you in my life."

"I think you've got me mixed up with someone else," she said. "I'd never seen you until I met you at the Forth of July picnic."

"Wrong," he hissed. "I might not be as skinny as I once was, I no longer wear glasses, and all those years I spent in Paris smoothed out the rough edges, but I'm still the same John Gagnon that took you to see Peter, Paul and Mary at the Assembly Hall. Do you remember that?"

"Yes. I do," she said her eyes wide in amazement. "We had a wonderful time."

"Why did you get pinned to that creep Pete Ryan the very next day then?" he snarled.

"Pete and I had been dating for months, but we had to do it secretively since the Kappa house had rules against the girls dating the waiters."

"How could you wear his pin if you had those rules?" he asked getting more and more agitated.

"He quit his job at the Kappa house and went to work for the Chi O's." she whispered staring at the gun in his shaky hand.

"O. K., O. K. That was then. This is now. I want you to pack your suitcase. You're coming with me."

"Where?" she asked choking back the tears.

"Anywhere. It's my turn to have you. I've waited long enough."

"No," she said. "I'm not leaving. This is my home now. If you want to go, you'll have to go without me."

He aimed the gun at her and warned her, "If I can't have you, no one can."

The sound of the doorbell ringing startled them both. As he jumped, his finger pulled the trigger and the gun went off. The bullet struck Connie in the chest and she crumpled to the floor. He glanced out the leaded window and saw Molly Donner standing at the front door. No way to escape. If he went down the stairway, she'd see him when he got to the bottom. He ran down the hall to a bedroom in the back of the house. The apple tree was just close enough. If he jumped he could grab that large branch and climb down. Thank goodness he had parked his car in The Four Aces parking lot. Just as he raised the window and pushed the screen out, he heard Molly open the front door and holler, "Yoo Hoo." He ran over to the bedroom door, closed and locked it, and headed back to the window. Good thing he had climbed a lot of trees as a kid he thought as he shinnied down the trunk and hit the ground running.

Chapter 46

"Yoo Hoo," she shouted as she poked her head in Connie's front door. "Anybody home?"

No answer.

"That's odd. I know I'm a little early, but I thought she'd be here." Molly thought as she walked through the living room toward the kitchen. She saw the cards neatly laid out on the dining room table and the crockpot bubbling away in the kitchen.

"Connie!" she said a little louder this time.

The doorbell rang again. As Molly opened the door to let Angie in, they heard a moan coming from upstairs.

"Maybe Connie's hurt up there." Molly said as she started toward the stairs. The moaning was coming from the Master Bedroom. They found Connie on the floor in a pool of blood. Molly bent down to see if she was breathing.

"Call 911," she said to Angie.

She picked up Connie's head and held it in her lap. As she gently touched her face Connie opened her eyes and whispered something.

"I'm sorry, Connie. I didn't hear you," Molly said as she bent down to hear better.

Gathering all her remaining strength, Connie said as loudly as she could, "John, not John," closed her eyes and died.

Molly continued to hold her until the paramedics arrived. She and Angie accompanied them to the hospital and called Pete and Ken from there.

Chapter 47

He landed on the ground, ran around the garage, and slipped down the slopping banks of the river stopping just short of the water. Crouching down so he couldn't be seen from the road, he had to decide what would be his next course of action. If he went toward the restaurant, some late lunchers might see him and wonder what he was doing there. He decided to head toward the golf course. He would have to pass Molly Donner's house and Emily Grant's house but he knew they would be at Connie's for bridge today so there was no danger of being seen there. He would slip into the locker room at the golf course where he could change out of his torn and muddy clothes into something clean that he kept there and he could also get some aspirin. His back and knees were beginning to ache from the 6-foot drop from the bottom branch of that damn tree. He was beginning to shake exactly like the day Beth died. Only this time, he didn't have his jacket on to keep him warm. Whatever happened to that thing? He couldn't have left it at the Stardust Motel, could he? He'd have to go back and look for it. What excuse could he give for going back? He'd have to think on that. Right now he needed a nap. He desperately needed a clear head so he could think what to do next.

Chapter 48

Tossing and turning all night long, Molly kept thinking about Connie's murder. She glanced at the bedside clock every twenty minutes. What could Connie have meant by "John not John"? Over and over she went over the happenings. How could the three murders be connected other than the victims all belonged to the Tuesday Bridge Club? Was it someone in the club that was jealous of their status in the community? Beth and Connie were relatively new to the community if you could call living there for fifteen years new. Nora had been there all her life. Beth and Connie were short; Nora was tall. All three were active in community affairs. All three were blonds. Blonds when they died, that is. Beth had only been blond a few hours. Her normally dark hair had been frosted at Jenny's the morning of her death. Jenny's. They were all regular customers there. Could it have been something they overheard while having their hair done? Something that someone did not want to get around? If so, then Jenny must've heard it too. Did that mean that Jenny was next on the list? After all, she was a member of the Tuesday Bridge Club too. Bridge. They were all killed by a bridge. What was the thread that connected all deaths?

"4:30," she read on the clock. "I've got to get some sleep." Just then she heard the screen door on the three seasons porch squeak as it slowly opened. Then she heard footsteps as someone crept across the room to the French doors leading to the family room. When she heard the glass break, she knew that whoever killed Connie was now after her. She got out of bed, pushed the pillows under the covers to resemble her body, slid her feet into a pair of old loafers, and put on her warm, fuzzy red robe that was lying on the cedar chest at the foot of her bed. No time to dress. She had to get out of there and get out fast. She peeked out the bedroom door and saw a shadowy figure come out of the bathroom and glide into Ken's old bedroom.

"He's not familiar with this house, thank goodness."

With that she closed her bedroom door and went through the walk-in closet to the bathroom. She hid in there peeking through a partly closed door praying that since he had already checked the bathroom he would not look there again. Soon she saw him leave Ken's room and go down the hall into her bedroom. Quietly she opened the door, tiptoed to the stairs, and silently crept down the carpeted stairway. She crossed the foyer, went through the kitchen and headed for the garage. Just as she reached the utility room, she heard two muffled shots coming from her room. Thinking that the pillows in the bed wouldn't fool him for long, she reached for her car keys on the hook near the back door. Gone. What to do now. She knew she couldn't outrun him and no one would be on the road to help her at this time of the morning. She entered the garage and looked frantically around for some form of transportation. The riding lawn mower was too loud and too slow. Tim and Tony's 10-speed bikes were too difficult to ride. Finally in desperation, she opened the door from the garage to the potting shed. It was very dark in there. Maybe she could hide under the work bench and he would be unable to find her. She reached her hand out, feeling her way in the dark. As she groped her way into the shed, her fingers felt the handle of the spade she had used to dig the geraniums down by the dock. Just then the door to the potting shed flew open and he stepped in breathing hard from running down the steps. It took him a minute for his eyes to get used to the darkness. As he hesitated, Molly's hands closed around the handle of the spade.

"It's now or never," she thought as she remembered Seth's instructions to Ken when he was learning to play baseball. "Bring the bat back, keep the swing level, transfer the weight to your front foot and follow through."

"WHACK!"

The spade hit the intruder squarely in the face. As he began to topple toward her, she retreated further into the shed. He landed with a plop on the floor and began to moan. As she tried to step past him, he grabbed her ankle with his hand. Quickly she picked up a large terra cotta pot from the work bench and crashed it against his head. She reached for a second pot to be sure he was knocked out. As he fell into unconsciousness, he released his grip. She jumped over the still form, picked up the spade where she had dropped it, closed the door to the potting shed, and wedged the handle of the spade through the door handle to prevent him from getting out. Then she ran into the kitchen and dialed 911. When Scott Miller answered, she gasped, "This is Molly Donner. Please send a car to my house. I have an intruder. Hurry! I think he's trying to kill me!"

"Dean's on patrol and just checked in from the High School. He should be at your house in five minutes." Scott replied. "I'll also call Ken and tell him to get right over there. In the meantime, are you all right? Can you get over to Mrs. Grant's?"

"Yes, yes," she panted into the phone. "Good idea! That's where I'll go."

Chapter 49

When Ken knocked on Emily Grant's door, Molly, Ben, and Emily were sitting at the kitchen table having coffee and talking over Molly's adventure.

"We found him in the potting shed out cold," said Ken as he sat down and accepted a cup of coffee from Emily. "He came to and we read him his rights before putting him in Dean's police cruiser and taking him to jail. He seemed pretty groggy, so I haven't had a chance to question him yet. Good thing you left your bedroom when you did, Mom. We found two slugs from a 38 in your pillows. We'll have the state police ballistics team see if they match the one that killed Connie Ryan."

"Well, who was it?" blurted out Molly.

"I thought it was going to be Rick James. When I arrested him last weekend, he had all that money on him and I thought he had stolen it from Beth's house. Turns out he won it at the race track up in Arlington Heights."

"Well, if it wasn't him, who was it?" asked Molly again.

"Jean-Claude Ganyo," replied Ken.

"Who?" the Grants and Molly said in unison.

"Jean-Claude Ganyo," repeated Ken. "You know, the new chef at the River Bend golf course."

"Why him?" asked Molly.

"I don't know. I guess we'll just have to find that out when we interrogate him in about an hour. Come on, I'll take you over to my house, Mom. Maybe now you can get some sleep."

Chapter 50

"Three hearts"

"Pass"

"Four hearts"

"Pass" "Pass" "Pass

"Pre-empt bids always make me nervous," thought Jenny as she scratched her newly died red hairdo. "I'm so used to starting at one and working my way up. It always scares me when my partner opens with three. It's a good thing I have four hearts in my hand. Otherwise I wouldn't have known what to answer."

The Tuesday Bridge Club was playing bridge in December contrary to their usual routine. But their lives had been anything but routine for the past several months. They usually skipped December due to busy schedules getting ready for Christmas, but because of Connie's death in November, they decided that they needed to get back to the comfort of the group. A now diminished group to be sure, but still wonderful old friends that had been together through thick and thin and would help each other through the murders of their friends.

"More tea, anyone?" asked Jenny as she moved from her place as dummy to the kitchen for refills. She had owned a three-story red brick building across Bridge Street from the Plush Pony. At first she had only used the first floor for her beauty shop, Clip

Joint. After she and her husband, Dennis, divorced several years ago, she and her two brothers gutted the second and third stories and made them into an adorable apartment. They left the outer walls brick, sanded and refinished the hardwood floors, hung chintz curtains from wooden rods to cover the floor-to-ceiling windows, and put up drywall to form new rooms. The kitchen with its cherry cabinets, the living room, the dining room, and one of the two bathrooms were on the second floor. Above them on the third floor were two bedrooms with a bath between them for her two boys and a master bedroom with a bath and walk-in closet for her across the entire front of the building. She had a great view of the main street and often sat on the window seat looking down at the town before she went to bed.

The living room couch was upholstered in blue chintz with little yellow and white flowers to match the curtains and the two companion chairs were solid blue to go along with the dominant color in the couch. On the floor of the living room and the dining room were braided rugs done in varying shades of blue. The walls that weren't brick had been painted white which helped brighten the rooms especially when the antique light fixtures hanging from the ten foot ceilings were on.

The balcony off the kitchen overlooked the municipal parking lot. In the summer Jenny hung baskets of impatiens from Petals and Pots from the rafters and filled flower boxes on the floor with petunias and marigolds. The redwood furniture there had thick cushions covered with yellow duck cloth. On warm sunny days, the Tuesday Bridge Club climbed the outer steps and walked across the balcony and into the kitchen. Today was cold and blustery with small hard pellets of snow driving their way earthward. The ladies were very glad to be able to take the elevator from Jenny's beauty shop up to her dining room.

"I'll have some tea," said Molly from the living room.

"Say, Molly," said Emily. "Did they ever figure out why Jean-Claude killed three people?"

"Ken said he confessed everything once he came to at the jail. Ken recommended that he call a lawyer, but he said he had to get it off his chest. The police called Arnold Metz to act as a public defender right away so that whatever Jean-Claude said could be used as evidence. Apparently, he was in love with Connie in college and was so broken hearted when she married Pete that he joined the Navy where he became a cook. On one tour of duty, he was stationed in France. He liked it so much, that when his hitch was up, he went back to study there. It was while he was living there that he changed his name to the French pronunciation. That's what Connie meant when she said to me, 'John not Jean.' "

"I read that there's lots of evidence to convict him. The motel owner said that he came there after Beth's death. He was so upset that he left his blood stained jacket on the floor between the bed and the wall," said Angie.

"Ken said Beth's murder was a mistake. He thought she was Connie because of her frosted hair. Then he poisoned Nora because he was afraid she saw him leaving Beth's. Rick James testified that he saw Jean-Claude come out of the tool shed at the ball game, but just didn't put two and two together until Jean-Claude was arrested. The police found Jean-Claude's fingerprints all over the box of arsenic in that tool shed," said Molly.

"Well, I hope they put him away for a long time," said Judy Philips. "What a horrible thing he did to this wonderful town. Killing three of the nicest ladies anywhere. People were afraid to go out, suspecting friends and neighbors. Why that nice Jimmy Reed at the gas station pumped my gas one day and I was afraid to even smile at him thinking maybe he was the one."

"I think we'll all sleep a lot better now that Jean-Claude's in jail. I know I will," said Molly.

"Oh, Molly. You're so brave. How did you ever think of hitting him with a spade?" said Peggy.

"I just used what was handy," she replied. "But it does seem like just desserts since he killed Beth with a club, Nora at the ball diamond, and shot Connie through the heart."

"He just messed with one too many of the Tuesday Bridge Club members," said Jenny as she dealt the cards around the table.

"One club"

"One heart"

"Two clubs"

"Pass" "Pass" "Pass"

About The Author

Merri Borkowski lives in the small northern Michigan town of Big Rapids. She and her husband, Bob, a retired football coach, have two sons, Brian and Casey. After graduating from the University of Illinois, Merri taught Business Education classes at the high school level for 30 years before becoming a licensed realtor. Growing up in a small town in Illinois provided Merri with life long friendships much like the women in the Tuesday Bridge Club.

Printed in the United States
64221LVS00001B/96

9 781418 408244